Peaceful War

Ali Reda Jeafar

First published by Dog Ear Publishing
4010 W. 86th Street, Ste H
Indianapolis, IN 46268
www.dogearpublishing.net

ISBN: 978-1-4575-1043-4

This book is printed on acid-free paper.

This book is a work of fiction. Places, events, and situations in this book are purely fictional and any resemblance to actual persons, living or dead, is coincidental.

Printed in the United States of America

INTRODUCTION PAGE

ON A DISTANT PLANET IN the Solion galaxy where the effect of time has not caught up with this world called Fortina. A 5 millennium war still drags on between the forces of Demaria and the Sinsorians, who are fighting in the name of the all powerful emperor Aaromir. They are fighting a war for peace that was started by the powers of greed. Now, Aaromir is the 5th emperor to lead the men against the soldiers of Demaria. Every millennium a new emperor is chosen to lead the men against their struggle with the legions of Demaria. Every Emperor lives until he is either slain or overthrown.

But Aaromir was different. He was beloved by the Sinsorians and the people of the Empire of Sinsoria. For that reason he is well protected and has lived for more than three millenniums. He commands vast armies of men, all who are willing to die in his name. Also Aaromir commands a massive army of knights, his most prized force, who are able to shake the ground with their march and who are able to wipe out any army just with their first charge. The men are all good warriors and are noble to the emperor and empire. But the Demarians despise the emperor and dream of one day burning the empire of Sinsoria to the ground.

CHAPTER 1

The Battle of the Old Brown Lands

THE DEMARIANS ARE BRUTAL, SAVAGE soldiers. Anyone not a native of Demaria was considered an enemy. They are a constant threat to the emperor. They are constantly attacking supply lines and raiding vulnerable villages. But, however, what they make up for in strength, they lose in number. Aaromir's armies outnumber the Demarians 5 to 1. However, the Sinsorians numbers do not ensure their victory since the Demarians are able to slaughter massive amounts of Sinsorians by mainly using small armies. The larger the Demarian force, the more Sinsorians they are able to kill. This makes the two forces evenly matched despite their many separate advantages and disadvantages. In battle, a single Demarian warrior is able to kill at least five Sinsorians before falling in battle. But, the constant massacre of their fellow brothers has not demoralized the Sinsorians at all. This is mainly because of their belief that to die in battle fighting for the emperor, means to live forever. As it is put by Ehandor, "It is better to die for the Emperor than to live for yourself". These are words of inspiration for all Sinsorians since they all truly believe in their true meaning. Ehandor is a fierce warrior of the emperor and one of his greatest leaders and warrior.

It has been five years since the major battle that gave the Sinsorians a new hope and will to fight. The battle ended with Ehandor vanquishing the Demarian champion and leader, Mithrandir: (he was the one who all the Sinsorians feared and dared not to face in battle since he was such a fierce warrior). Upon defeating Mithrandir, the men of Sinsoria gained a new hope and the Demarian forces were left in turmoil. This allowed the Sinsorians to divide the demarian forces all across the planet. With the division of the Demarian forces, Ehandor was given leadership of the Sinsorian forces, and ever since then, he has done wonders with the Sinsorians, gaining them many crucial victories against their lifelong enemies. The Sinsorians believe that with leaders like Ehandor and an emperor like Aaromir, they can finally achieve the peace they have long sought and fought for. Aaromir shares this dream as well. For this reason, he is striking at weak, vulnerable Demarian targets such as supply villages and weak armies to help rid the world of Demarian tyranny. But, the Demarians have developed an unbelievable hatred towards the emperor and only have revenge in their minds and hatred in their hearts.

While weak forces are being destroyed by their enemies and their ability to launch a fully fledged offense is greatly restricted, stronger Demarian forces are attacking settlements and shrines built to praise the emperor. After months of these attacks, Ehandor decided to meet with Aaromir to discuss the issue.

"We cannot keep ignoring these attacks my lord."

"I know, but the men are battle weary and beaten, there is little I can do at the moment" expressed Aaromir.

"Then let me lead an army to fight off the attackers and save our lands" proclaimed Ehandor.

"But where will you get your troops? There is a large Demarian army marching towards the city of Theriodon. They have all ready burnt several villages and homes belonging to the farmers and slaughtered hundreds of people. If they are not stopped at the Old Brown lands then our entire food supply will be crippled and the men and citizens of Sinsoria will starve. The main army has already been sent to stop this Demarian army in the far north, while the rest are dealing with raids to the south and west. I can't risk sending out our forces stationed within the walls because that would leave all of Sinsoria defenseless. I have already sent word to our forces stationed in the east and they cannot help us since they are dealing with stiff Demarian resistance all across the area. "

"Then who is left?" asked Ehandor doubtedly.

"Only men I can spare are the royal and town guards. They are well trained but have no experience in battle, they are loyal and high spirited, they will stand by you in battle and will do whatever it takes to defend their lands and fight for the empire." assured Aaromir.

“Being well trained and high spirited won’t help much in our struggle to defeat the Demarian forces.” Indicated Ehandor regrettably, “Nevertheless, I will prepare the men for battle.”

“Very well then, you have three months to prepare the men as best you can.” declared Aaromir.

“Three months?! But my lord I will need more time! Three months is not enough!” protested Ehandor.

“That’s all we have, within three months the Demarians will be outside the walls. They’d be here sooner if I hadn’t already sent word out to the forces near the Demarians. They have agreed to slow them down the best they can, sadly however, they lack the strength to fight off the Demarian force, and three months is all the time they can buy us. Any longer than that will be impossible since they are already dangerously undermanned.”

“I’ll see what I can do” replied Ehandor, then left to begin training the men.

Just as he left a town’s woman came to pay her taxes.

“Why has your husband not come to pay the tax?” asked Aaromir.

“He is ill, my lord, and is unable to leave his bed at the moment.” Expressed the woman

“I will send a few healers over to your house to see if they can make your husband well again” proclaimed Aaromir.

“Thank you my lord.” replied the woman.

“My lord, if you don’t mind me asking, why are we fighting the demarians? Why are our men, husbands, sons, and friends dying?” Aaromir was silent for a moment. Then he replied, "It is because the war has gotten fiercer and the Demarians refuse to give us our peace. They will not stop until we are all dead."

"But my lord, what started the war?" asked the woman. Aaromir let out a sigh then began "It all started in the time of the first emperor, Emperor Niastros. During the beginning of his rein he and the Demarians were mighty allies. They had vanquished many foes and built a massive kingdom. But the mightiest of their enemies were the Philosphers, rich and powerful warriors who were in control of a massive kingdom. The Philosophers had been fighting Niastros and the Demarians for twenty years.

Then, finally, their reign and kingdom was brought to an end by their own greed when they managed to steal the ancient stone of the Demarians, which caused the Demarians to go into a frenzy and throw everything they had at the Philosphers. Upon seeing that the Demarians needed reinforcements, and a chance to bring down a powerful enemy, Niastros decided to come to the aid of his mighty ally. And together, they overran the Philosopher's defenses and took control of the kingdom and burnt it into the ground.

After the Philosphers were destroyed Niastros and the Demarians gathered up the treasures and gold that was found in the kingdom and split it amongst one another, with the Sinsorians getting the larger half since they needed it more and all the Demarians really cared about was getting their ancient stone back, which they did. A year later, the Demarians and Sinsorians continued to dominate, destroy, and eliminate all other races since the other races got in the way of their plans for expansion. Both the Sinsorians and Demarians had a dream to expand their empires all across the planet and control all of the land and be the most powerful empire in history. When the war of expansion was over, only the Demarians and Sinsorians remained. For a while there was peace.

Then one day, the Demarians decided that they had not received a fair share of the gold that had been plundered and pillaged from the other kingdoms. So they went to Niastros and asked him to give them more gold to even out their amounts. Niastros agreed to the terms, he thought they were reasonable, and gave them their share and used the rest to start our empire of Sinsoria from the ruins of the destroyed kingdoms. There was still enough left to support the empire. But then the Demarians became consumed with greed and wanted more gold, this was five years after they had received their fair share, and again asked Niastros to give them more gold. “I had already given you your share, and I need the rest to support my empire and give to my people. I’m sorry I cannot give you more gold.” The Demarians were baffled. They asked again, they were turned down again.

They asked three more times, they were turned down every time. Niastros began to lose patience. He warned the Demarians not to ask again, for he would never give them more gold. (By this time Sinsoria had been fully constructed and Niastros had taken his place as emperor.) The Demarians had become furious. They began to raid shipments of gold and take it for themselves. Niastros tried ignoring these raids for a year, in order to preserve the peace and the friendship he had long shared with the Demarians, but could ignore it no longer when the people began to starve and riot since they could not afford to but the high priced food. At first, food prices were so low, all could buy as much as they wanted, and there was plenty to go around. But as the supply of gold became short, many town folks didn’t have the money to buy the food as prices rose to make sure there was an income for stores to stay open. So Niastros sent an army to stop these attacks. The soldiers fought off the Demarian raids, but it cost them many lives.

Niastros then decided to meet with the Demarians to arrange a truce. At the meeting war was declared instead of a cease fire. It was Niastros's last declaration since he was then slain by Nichrangon, the Demarian champion at the time. The men were infuriated and launched an assault on the Demarians who were moving in to pillage a settlement in the Apahalo Mountains. That was the first battle of the war.

It ended with a draw, but that is what began the endless slaughter of men and Demarians for the many battles to come afterward as the war drew out and escalated. We have been fighting ever since." ended Aaromir with a sigh.

"But my lord, why can't we call a peace now?" asked the townswoman in confusion.

"There have been too many deaths on both sides for us to even consider the thought of peace. We both now only have revenge in our minds. The only way to end this war now, is to kill every last Demarian that still draws breath. That will ensure our victory." The towns woman then nodded with satisfaction and thanked the emperor for what he has told her about the war's history and left. Meanwhile, Ehandor had already met with the royal and town guards and explained the current situation with the Demarian armies in Theriodon and how they must be stopped at the Old Brown Lands or they will be outside the walls of Sinsoria.

"But how can we stop the Demarians? They are incredibly skilled warriors and are more powerful than we are!" argued Kenneth of the royal guards. Ehandor looked at him and proclaimed "First off, it's not a matter of if we can stop the Demarians but a manner of what would happen if we don't stop them. Beyond Theriodon do you know what lies there?

Farms, villages, cattle, livestock-our food supply. If they are not stopped then the farmers would be killed, villages burnt, cattle and livestock slaughtered. That's just the beginning, with the destruction of the farms, Sinsoria will lose its food supply and its sons and daughters will starve. The men defending its borders will become weak and soon enough, all of Sinsoria will fall. You are all that stands between Sinsoria and its destruction. So are you with me?" asked Ehandor. The men did not answer. Ehandor asked again "Are you WITH ME?!" yelled Ehandor.

The men all burst into a loud cheer and that was when Ehandor knew that they were with him until the end, the men had the knowledge of what they were fighting for. Then began the intensive training. Ehandor trained the men and pushed them harder than any other group of men he had ever trained. He pushed them to their limits and beyond, to a point where they actually believed they could defeat the Demarians. This is a critical physiological state because it gives the men a will to fight and fight hard. It was also a point that Ehandor had to reach within the three months because without it, there would be no chance of victory.

All other men and armies took years to reach this point, so Ehandor was off to a great start, mostly because Ehandor had not pushed his past armies as hard as he is pushing the royal and town guards now. When the three months were over, Ehandor's men were ready for anything, so he took his army of 200,000 men to the Old Brown Lands. When they reached the lands, the Demarians had just begun to advance into the region. Both armies had advanced half way into the lands when they each stopped in their tracks. The armies were staring now at each other. The Demarians saw that they were heavily outnumbered but held their ground, all 80,000 of them.

The men saw the Demarians; they were shocked at the appearance of their opponents. They saw heavily armored soldiers in silver armor that were twice their size but smaller in number. Then there was silence. No one breathed, no one spoke, both armies just continued to stare in dead silence. Then a cry broke out, it was Ehandor rousing the men and breaking the silence:"FOR THE EMPEROR!!"

The men broke out in a scream and charged full speed at the Demarians. The Demarians saw the men charging and one solider lifted his sword above his head and thrust it forward; letting out a scream after the thrust, and the Demarians began charging at the men. Both armies ran full speed at the other. The men continued screaming and knew that all their training had prepared them for this moment. The armies then collided; armor smashing against armor, shield against shield, and sword against sword. The deafening sound echoed across the land. Ehandor had swung his sword in the waist and stomach area of a Demarian and turned and punched another demarian next to the one he just killed.

Men were screaming, muskets firing, and men flipping over at the collision of the armies. Swords mashing against shields, armor clanking as it hit the ground, swords tearing through flesh, swords breaking against sword, it was an all out battle. The men used their numbers to kill the Demarians; three men would take on one Demarian. For the most part it would work and a Demarian would fall, but some Demarians killed all three men and moved on to kill three more men before falling in battle. Musketeers gathered together in order to mow down advancing Demarians in barrages of musket fire. Ehandor was killing many Demarians by himself, a one man army. He would lung his sword in one demarian and then turn and stabs another, then slices a third one and knock a fourth one to the ground and cut him at the neck. Seeing their leader slaying the enemy would give the men more moral to fight. The men slowly began to defeat the Demarians. Ehandor kept urging the men to fight harder and fight on. Victory was within reach.

Then Ehandor saw something...he saw Kenneth alone surrounded by Demarians. He was fighting bravely, and was vanquishing many foes. When suddenly a demarian warrior had come from behind and knocked him down to the floor. Then two more demarians came and one placed his foot on Kenneth and held him down while the other one stood in front of him and lifted his sword high above his head, ready to strike it down. Ehandor yelled and charged sword drawn, and killed the one Demarian holding Kenneth down and plunged his sword into the heart of the one in front of him and pulled it out as the Demarian fell. As he was turning around a slash rang out, Ehandor stood there...paralyzed, then placed his hand on his chest and took it off to see his hand covered in blood. In front of him he saw the Demarian who had just slashed him, still in holding his sword to the side of his body as blood dripped from it.

Ehandor stabbed his sword into the Demarinan's chest and forced it through, then withdrew it. He tried to turn towards Kenneth but was stopped halfway by three swords lunging into his stomach. Three Demarians stood towering in front of him. Ehandor lifted his sword and slashed it at the soldier on the right, then the one on the left, killing them both. Then with all his strength he grabbed the handle of the sword held by the Demarian in front of him and pulled it further within him, grunting in pain as he did it. He then gave a scream and another as he lifted his sword and a third and final scream as he drove his sword into the chest of the Demarian, afterward Ehandor dropped to his knees.

A fourth Demarian came from behind and lifted sword, ready to strike, but was shot down by a group of ten musketeers.

Ehandor then surveyed the battle, saw many dead Demarians and many more dead men, and he seen the fighting that was going on. He also saw his men, the royal and town guards, fighting the Demarians and winning, then he knew that he had trained them well, he fell backwards then died. Upon seeing Ehandor fall the men broke into a frenzy and charged at the Demarians like mad men, Kenneth leading them, and killing off the demarian horde. The demarians that tried to run were shot down by the musketeers. The battle was over and the men had won, but at a heavy price. Out of the 200,000 that charged into battle, only 80,000 remained, among the dead was Ehandor.

The men want back to Sinsoria and were greeted by cheering soldiers and town's people. They have saved the empire and were commended by Aaromir himself for their bravery and service. On that day of celebration there was also grief, for Ehandor had fallen, and he was to be remembered. He was taken to Fania, the burial area of all fallen heroes. Upon those who buried him was Kenneth, the man he had saved. Not all was bad however; more good news had come from the other army that was sent to fight off the massive Demarian horde in the northern lands. They were victorious and the raids in the south were put down. However, with the death of Ehandor, one of the greatest leaders, Aaromir knew that the war was far from over. Until the legions of Demaria had can be driven from the planet, the war still drags on. Also the peace they have long sought but never found was still far away, and would not come within reach for many years to come.

CHAPTER 2

Replacing a once great leader

WITH THE DEATH OF EHANDOR, Aaromir knew that he had to find someone to replace Ehandor as leader. So he sent out a message to all men, all throughout Sinsoria. His message was simple but demanding: "Our brother Ehandor has fallen fighting for the peace we have been working so hard to achieve. I now seek a man who will take Ehandor's place as a strong leader and lead Sinsoria's sons to victory." When the message got out, there was no shortage of volunteers. The Sinsorians all wanted a chance to lead their brethren into battle against the demarians. Many men came to prove their loyalty and test their worthiness to the emperor. However, many men were turned down. Their skills were not what Aaromir was looking for. He needed a leader who had extreme courage and hope, even among impossible odds, a leader who would be willing to sacrifice himself for the empire in order to bring hope and moral for all other men and further encourage them to fight on against their enemies. This leader would also have to be powerful, and be able to vanquish many foes before falling in the battle field. Aaromir wanted a leader who has, respect for himself along with respect for all other men. Also to be a genius when it comes to skill in arms and tactics in the battlefield against the full faced knight helmed, cape wearing, heavily armored demarians.

Most men lacked the skill, let alone bravery, that Aaromir is searching for. There was one warrior who had all the qualities except one, which was having the respect for the other men. Aaromir told this man that without this respect, which is something he will not tolerate by his leaders or anyone in command, the Sinsorians would not obey his orders and leave him to die. "My lord," said the soldier, "I can assure you that I am more than capable of standing on my own. I will lead no armies and achieve the peace we have been fighting for single handedly. I don't need an army," were Spehachor's last words to the emperor. Spehachor is the most self-centered men in all of Sinsoria, which was something Aaromir despised the most about him. And for him to merely utter the words "single handedly" and "I don't need an army" is an act of defiance to Aaromir's ears.

Aaromir stood up from his throne and screamed at Spehachor: "Be silent fool! You know not what you are saying! GUARDS! Take this selfish fool out of my sight! Teach him to show respect for his brothers and learn how to work with others to achieve a goal!" The guards grabbed Spehachor's and dragged him outside.

"You're making a mistake my lord!"Informed Spehachor, "I am Sinsoria's weapon, I am your fist, and I am all what keeps this empire from falling to the demarians!"

"You're wrong," said Aaromir "Sinsoria's sons and my brothers are what keep the demarians at bay and keep all thoughts they might have of attacking Sinsoria out of their minds."

Spehachor was then thrown down the stone steps that lead to Aaromir's throne room.

Shortly after Spehachor had been "escorted" out of the throne room, a nobleman approached Aaromir and asked to be the new leader of Sinsoria's armies.

"Why should you be leader, when all other men have been turned down?" asked Aaromir, "What makes you more superior than other men?"

"If you give me a chance my lord, I can show you my skills and then let you decide if I am worthy or not," answered the nobleman.

"Very well," sighed Aaromir "You may proceed." The nobleman then showed the emperor what he can do and all the skills and tactics he knows. Aaromir was astounded at what he was seeing, he did not believe that there was actually someone who could replace Ehandor, but this nobleman had surpassed all of Aaromir's expectations with enormous vigor. When the nobleman finished, Aaromir could not help but applaud this young nobleman.

"Bravo, bravo, young noblemen" cheered Aaromir, "Where ever did you learn such skills, such, such, technique or develop these tactics, attack and defensive formations.

This is skill worthy of recognition, tell me what is your name?" asked Aaromir curiously.

"Aloysius sire."

"Well Aloysius you certainly have the skills and the appearance of a leader I can give you that."

"Thank you my lord."

"Who taught you your skills Aloysius?"

"No one my lord, I just watched the soldiers training and studied their movements and practiced them on my own, and added a little spice and creativity to each technique and skill that I learn."

"Impressive, and your father didn't help you with any of this?"

"No my lord, I live with my mother, I don't have a father anymore."

"Why not what happened?"

"He was killed when I was a little boy by the demarians. You might remember him, his name was Becnivor."

"Ah, yes I remember him, he was a fine warrior. You should be proud."

"I am, my lord, which is why I have come here to avenge my father's death and fight alongside my brothers on the battle field against our foes."

"I can personally guarantee you that your father will be avenged," assured Aaromir, "So tell me what is your mother's name if you don't mind me asking?"

"Farah, my lord, my mother's name is Farah."

“Very well then, go tell Farah that emperor Aaromir has found his new leader, and he is a young man with black hair, brown eyes, a sword at his right side, a silver plate of armor, leg guards, and is wearing black gloves, does not carry a shield or a helmet but is wearing black shoes, but has no facial hair. Also tell her that his name is Aloysius.”

Aloysius thanked Aaromir for the honor he has given him and ran off crying tears of joy.

This young man who is only 24 years old, and has no father, was given the title of leader of Aaromir’s armies. An honor he will cherish for the rest of his life, no matter how short it might be.

CHAPTER 3:

The Emperor's Fist

WHEN ALOYSIUS WAS GIVEN THE title of leader, the first thing he did was run straight home to tell his mother, who was washing dishes outside of their small house.

"Mother, mother, "cried Aloysius, "I have fantastic news!"

"What is it?" asked Farah curiously, "What has you so excited? Did you ask the emperor if you could be leader?"

"Yes I did and you'll never guess what happened when I showed him my skills."

"What?"

“I showed Aaromir my skills and tactics and guess what happened next.”

“What? Tell me.”

“I got the position, you are now looking at the new leader of Sinsoria’s armies,” said Aloysius. Farah was speechless for a while. Then she got up, and let out a scream of joy and hugged and kissed her son. She held him tight as tears of joy poured from her eyes. They then danced around for a long while, singing and laughing, and then went inside their house to have a feast in order to celebrate this incredible honor.

Meanwhile, Spehachor was watching them from a nearby watchtower, and then said to himself, “It should have been me, and it should have been me. Aaromir will regret not giving the leader position to me. He will pay for this; I’ll make sure of it.” Then he disappeared into the watchtower. After three days of celebration with friends and family, Aloysius went to meet the troops that he would be leading. He went into the barracks where all leaders go to get their recruits. It’s the barracks where all fresh troops awaited their leaders to recruit them. When Aloysius entered the barracks, all the other leaders had already taken the men that they needed for their armies.

None however, were Aloysius’s men. He wondered around asking where his men were. None were his, and no one knew where his men were, because he did not know their names and ranks. Then messenger, sent by Aaromir, told him that the emperor had requested him in the Solaris barracks, where all the most powerful and highly skilled warriors were, because of their skill and brute strength and force, they are nicknamed “The Emperor’s Fist”. So Aloysius went to the Solaris barracks, which was on the third highest level of Sinsoria. When he got there, he saw Aaromir standing in front of huge, heavily armored, full faced helmed, strong men with humongous weapons that were too heavy for the normal Sinsorians to hold, let alone keep in their sword sheathes. It takes 50 Sinsorians, using both hands, just to lift the weapons two feet off the ground. These powerful soldiers were able to lift these weapons with only one hand. In the other hand they carried shields, huge, arm breaking shields.

Their shields are able to protect a man from head to toe, and a demarian from thigh to neck. The name of these massive warriors was the Trocarians. These were men beyond any other. A single Trocarian is able to go toe to toe with a demarian and have half a chance of winning compared to the single Sinsorians, who had a quarter of a chance. The Trocarian numbers are equal to that of the demarians, but they slightly outnumber them 2 to 1. These barbarians are the main reason that keeps the thoughts of attacking Sinsoria out of the minds of the demarians. Just to see a Trocarian kill or simply wound a demarian, gives the Sinsorians a huge reason to fight on and more moral to stay in the fight longer.

When Aloysius was told that he would be the leader of these brutes, he was shocked and astounded.

"My lord, I, I, I, don't think I can do this." stuttered Aloysius doubtedly.

"I am intrusting you with this task because I believe that you are the one who can do it," commented Aaromir.

"But lord Aaromir, you have entrusted me with a very important task and I don't, I can't do it. Maybe if I were to be given a less demanding position? What about the Corics?" asked Aloysius.

"The Corics's training is not complete and they are raw recruits and have had no contacts with the fields and foes outside the walls. Besides, these men (pointing at the Trocarians) are leaderless and eager to get back into battle. But I cannot send them into battle without a leader. You are the only one who has ever shown such skills. This is perfect for someone like you. What do you say? Are you up for it?" asked Aaromir. Aloysius thought for a while and then answered: "Yes. I am up for it." Aaromir smiled then confided "Excellent. You must make yourself worthy of this task in the Citcon temple on the highest level of Sinsoria. You can't lead the Trocarians in your current form."

So Aloysius climbed the mountain and made it to the Citcon temple. It was there that a Sinsorians can become a Trocarian by going through the Trojan trials. The Trojan Trials are a series of brutal tests that destroy a person's mind and body and replace them with a body and mind one can only dream of having. When the Trials are complete, a Sinsorians's original body is a shadow of his current form. Muscles, larger and beyond what one's mind can comprehend, a mental thinking capability that makes the smartest Sinsorians look like a three year old child. And the size and width of these people, is just simply mind boggling. Aloysius partook in these trials for seven months. Every day he would return to Farah broken and battered, but the next day he would force himself up the mountain and continue his intense training. He would then return home more broken and battered than the day before.

Farah became very worried about her son's well being and began to beg him to reconsider. She tried to make him stay home just to rest, but he was persistent and went to the Trojan trials regardless of his mother's best efforts to make stay home and rest. He told her that this is the only way he can prove his worthiness in taking on the task of leading the Trocarians to victory and avenge his father. Aloysius then began to notice his body was undergoing a transformation.

His arms began to feel stronger, his bones began to crack and turn to dust and larger, stronger, wider bones took their place. His muscles began to over grow and build up around the bones. The pain began to slowly drift away, and he felt himself becoming immune to the pain and punishment that his body was forced to withstand. Aloysius also found himself growing taller than everyone else. And he noticed that he began to think on a higher mental capacity, one higher than everyone else. This was the mentality of the Trocarians, which allowed all Trocarians to think quickly and rationally under pressure or in the heat of battle. Aloysius grew so tall and large that to simply enter his small home became a problem as he grew every day. Farah was then forced to buy a new, larger house; with a larger doorway with the gold she had been given by Aaromir in order to ensure that Aloysius continues his training. Farah had never thought to buy a larger because she saw no need for a larger house since it was mainly her and her son. But because her son had grown so large, she didn't really have a choice.

After the seven months of the Trojan Trails, the thing everyone thought possible became possible, Aloysius had become a Trocarian. His muscles have grown so large that they overlapped and wrapped around his bones. He was twice times the size of an average man and he was able to hold the Halberd of Purification, his weapon of choice out of the armory designed specifically for the leaders of the Trocarians. This weapon is the heaviest of all the Trocarian weapons and is the second most powerful weapon bellow Aaromir's Sword of Kings. (The Halberd is an enchanted weapon that is only given to the worthiest and most powerful warriors. Aloysius was proud and overwhelmed with joy to find out that he was worthy enough to hold this weapon). The pain had completely vanished from his mind, but not his body. The pain was still there, greater than ever before. His body is incredibly sore and in an excruciating amount of pain. He had just become the pain, which allowed his mind to simply "cancel" it out.

It was now time for Aloysius to put on his armor. He was led into the armory to the Trocarian section for his armor fitting. The plate and leg guards were chosen for him, while he chose his weapon and helmet of choice. The Halberd of Purification was Aloysius's automatic weapon since it had already chosen him. His helmet took him a while to find. There were so many to choose from, most of which looked exactly the same as all the others. There were only ten helmets that were separate from all the rest. All of which were already taken by the ten captains who are second highest in command below Aloysius. However, they must follow his commands.

The helmet that Aloysius chose was the one that no one else thought he would pick. As he was browsing the countless aisles of helmets, he came across one helmet that was alone on a stone stand in the heart of all the aisles. As Aloysius looked around all the aisles emptied out into this one area, then Aloysius's eyes met the eyes of the empty helmet. This helmet had once belonged to the original Trocarian leader and the one who first created the Trocarians. Once he passed away his helmet was placed on the stand. Before it was placed, the leader had proclaimed "Let this helmet not be lifted from this stand of stone, lest the one, who claims it, be able to stand alone."

As Aloysius examined the ancient warning, he took a moment to understand what it was intended for. He then looked on the stone stand that had the warning carved onto it. He then remembered the rumors of a helmet that could not be lifted off a stone stand, no matter how hard it was pulled. Then Aloysius remembered what one of the clerks had told him before he began the Trojan trials. He confessed,

"To become a Trocarian you must be able to stand with your brothers. If you are unable to stand by your brothers than you cannot wield the power weapons, you cannot wear the heavy armor; you will not be able to survive the trials. The Trocarians act and move as one powerful force. If one falls, another must quickly take his place lest they all fall.

To be the leader, however, involves you being able to move and act with the force with absolute precision. The most important thing to take into deep consideration is that if the force is broken, if the Trocarians are all dead, if your brothers have deserted you, then you alone must continue the fight regardless of the odds against you. You must not retreat nor surrender for any reason. For if you do than you will lose the rank of leader and be forever exiled among your friends, family, and be forever cursed for breaking the line of leaders in all of Trocarian history, who died fighting alone."

"Fighting alone, stand alone, exiled, cursed for breaking the chain," these words rung and spun around in Aloysius's thoughts as he looked at the helmet. He then reached slowly, cautiously, ever so cautiously, for the helmet. As Aloysius reached for the helmet, the words of the clerk could still be heard in his ears as if he was standing next to him, uttering those words over and over.

When Aloysius's hands had reached the helmet, he put one hand on the right side and the other hand on the left side. Then he gave a gentle tug, and the helmet easily lifted off the stone stand. It was at that moment that Aloysius knew that he had become worthy of being a leader and can finally avenge his father's death. Astounded by his own accomplishments, Aloysius lifted the full-faced helmet high above his head, and stared at it with joy.

"All that pain, all those long days of training and becoming stronger, have all led me to this moment in destiny, I dare not delay it any longer." admonished Aloysius to himself. He then lowered the helmet to his head, picked up his Halberd of Purification and gripped it tightly with both hands. He then headed towards the exit of the armory where Aaromir and the other Trocarians were waiting for him.

As soon as Aloysius stepped out and everyone saw his armor and weapon, Aaromir cracked a smile while the other Trocarians let out a huge cheer. They knew now that after 300 years of defending Sinsoria, they would finally be able to fight for Sinsoria. For it is by Trocarian law that they cannot take the fields and fight unless there is a leader present to lead them. When the last leader passed away 300 years ago, the Trocarians had become a defense force rather than an attack force.

Now they can finally take the field and once again fight the demarians up close. Just in time as well, for Aaromir has just informed Aloysius of a demarian army wreaking havoc on the Western lands.

"If they are not stopped, I am afraid many lives will be lost," acknowledged Aaromir. "You must take the Trocarians and stop this army before they progress further into the Western lands." Aloysius nodded, rallied his troops and began marching, all 50,000 of them. As they marched, the Sinsorians cheered. To see the Trocarians marching in perfect unison, all together, no one a step behind or a step ahead, filled the men with joy as they cheered them on.

After several hours of marching the Trocarians reached the western lands just as the demarians began progressing further in. The demarians halted at the first sight of the Trocarians marching towards them. They never thought that they would face the Trocarians again after their last encounter 300 years ago. They were surprised to see them again, and with a new leader as well. When the Trocarians had marched to the center of the region, Aloysius told them to stop.

He knew that this was his chance of finally avenging his father. As the two armies stared at one another, they realized that they were evenly matched. Man for man, numbers would not play an advantage in this fight. Aloysius realizing this turned to his brethren: "Trocarians," announced Aloysius calmly. The Trocarians did not answer. They were focused on their enemy, eager to fight. They began to tighten their grips on their weapons and shields.

"TROCARIANS!" yelled Aloysius. Then all in unison, they all straightened up and pounded their fists on their plates in a salute and one boasted in a heroic, courages voice, "The emperor's finest" (salutes)"ready for war."

"FOR THE EMPEROR!" hollered Aloysius. The Trocarians then gave a cheer and charged at the demarians. When the demarians seen the Trocarians charging, they didn't know what to do and stood right where they were, too frightened to move.

The demarians stood motionless until one solider broke this fear by pointing his sword at the Trocarians, and charged. The others seen him charging and shook their fear and charged as well. Now both armies were running full speed at one another. Aloysius was leading the Trocarians while the demarians were leaderless. Aloysius was a few steps ahead of the Trocarians. The armies got closer and closer to one another. Right before they collided, Aloysius had swung his halberd into the stomach area of a demarian. The impact was so great that the demarian was lifted off the ground, dieing as he went up and died when he hit the floor. The force that Aloysius had put into his strike was so powerful, that it drove the halberd through the air and cut the demarian, the one behind the first one, in half at the waist. Then the two armies collided and a huge echo of armor colliding rung out. A Trocarian smashed his smashes his shield against a demarian, then lunged his massive sword all the way through him and pulled it back out then turned and sliced another demarian at the neck and continued fighting.

Another Trocarian was charging at a demarian while the demarian was fighting another Trocarian. The demarian killed the Trocarian he was fighting then turned to see the one Trocarian running at him. The demarian acts fast and shoves his sword into the waist of the charging Trocarian. The impact was strong enough to stop the charging Trocarian and have him drop his weapon, but not strong enough to kill him, let alone seriously injure him. The Trocarian stood motionless for a few seconds as the pain came, then vanished as quickly as it came. After the Trocarian just simply ignores the pain and grabs the demarian and head butts him. The hit was so great that the demarian let go of his sword and backed off extremely dizzy.

The Trocarian quickly capitalizes and pulls the sword out from his waist and stabs it through the dazed demarian warrior. Since he was much stronger and stabbed it through the stomach of the demarian, the demarian died as soon as the Trocarian pulled the blade back out. When he pulled it out and the demarian fell, the Trocarian saw another demarian charging at him. As he got closer the Trocarian lifted up the demarian blade and slashed it at the charging demarian's leg. The power he had put into the slash was so powerful that the demarian was lifted off the ground. While he was in the air, the demarian saw his leg separated from his body and land a few feet away. The Trocarian then brought the sword handle down on the demarian with such force that he smashed against the ground so hard that he became paralyzed for a few seconds. The Trocarian wasted no time, he then quickly spun the sword around so the blade was facing downward, and then forced it through the demarian on the ground with both hands on the handle.

Aloysius was just unleashing his rage on the demarians. When he sliced a demarian with his halberd, he would waste no time and quickly go after another demarian. As he was fighting, one demarian tried attacking him from behind. Aloysius saw this demarian approaching and lifted his halberd and struck down on the head of the demarian in front of him, splitting open his helmet and splattering his blood all over Aloysius's armor. Then just as the demarian behind Aloysius had lifted his sword ready to strike it down, Aloysius elbowed him in the chest. After he brought his hand up so his knuckles hit the demarian's helmet, then he brought his hand down so the fingers hit the demarian's lower chest. After he brings his elbow up and hits the demarian's chin. The demarian then stepped backward, dazed and trying to regain focus. Aloysius did not give him the time however. When the demarian had stepped back, Aloysius had gripped his halberd with both hands. He lifted it, turned swiftly, and then brought the halberd down on the demarian's head, hearing the cracking sound of his skull shattering under the incredible force of his weapon. The blow forced the lifeless carcass of the demarian to the ground, with the halberd lodged with in the skull.

Aloysius pulled the halberd up and urged the other Trocarians to continue fighting.

"Onward my brothers, FOR THE EMPIRE!!" The Trocarians regrouped and charged at the remaining demarians, with Aloysius in the lead. After a few more minutes of fighting, the Trocarians stood victorious. Out of the 50,000 that charged into battle, 10,000 lay dead. A great victory for the Trocarians and a substantial victory for Aloysius. This was his first battle against the demarians and he was overwhelmed with joy at his victory. He had slaughtered many demarians but still feels that he hasn't avenged his father's death. As he stepped forward to survey the battlefield, he saw that all the demarians that had charged into battle, lying dead on the floor. When he reached the end of the battle field, he turned to look at his army. There was silence for a while before all the Trocarians burst into a cheer. At first Aloysius was surprised, then he realized that they were all cheering for him. This was the first time they have gone into battle in 300 years and could think of no better way to come out of a battle: victorious. While under Aloysius's leadership, the Trocarians believed that there will be many more victories to come.

CHAPTER 4

The battle of the Olditron Canyons

FARAH WATCHED THE FIELDS OF Sinsoria for any sight of an approaching army from her large doorway. It was the first time Aloysius had ever been outside the walls and beyond the ever watchful eyes of the tower guards.

"Be safe," she muttered to herself," For the love of the emperor, be safe." Farah continued to watch helplessly as time passed by.

"Everything alright mistress?" asked a mysterious voice. When Farah turned around, she saw Aaromir towering behind her.

"Is everything alright?" asked Aaromir again. Just the sight of the emperor filled Farah with an unbelievable amount of hope and made her forget her worries.

Speechless for a short time and overtaken by a sense of loyalty, Farah could hardly think of anything to say then finally managed to stutter out,

"No, everything is fine my lord."

"Why do you ask?" chuckled Farah nervously.

"You seem troubled, I noticed you standing here from the small grassland to the throne room" (he points upward to a very high open plain that lies on top of a flattened stone mountain). "I sensed that you were worried seeing how you stare out into the open fields like that," acknowledged Aaromir.

"It's just my son, he's in the army and it's his first time outside the walls. I'm just worried about his safety that's all," recalled Farah.

"Ah I see," indicated Aaromir, "There's always a worry when it comes to loved ones. It happens to all of us, no matter how many times a son, father, uncle, grandfather, or whoever leaves the safety of the walls. There's always that fear of them never returning. Everyone that dies is a blow from the death hammer on the nail of Sinsoria. We need all the men we can get if we ever want to have the hope of one day defeating the demarians and finally achieve the peace we have been fighting for.

It's not easy being emperor; you have to make decisions for the well being of everyone, even if it means sending their loved ones to their death. Every day I wonder if I am making the right decisions with the men. Every time I send them out into battle, I see the floor begin to flood with the tears of the families and widows. To see the men not come back and those same families weep over the fallen family members, it darn near breaks my heart. I just sometimes wish the pain would ease just a little so I don't feel so heartless. There's no way I can feel better if more and more men are dying each day. The townspeople then come to me, with eyes blind with tears. Sometimes I don't even have the heart to face them. There's just no break in the rainfall of tears," expressed Aaromir.

Just then a watchman on the wall sent out a yell "TROCARIANS!!!! The Trocarians are returning!!!" Then the gate guards ran to their positions. They all made it and began unlocking the locks. Chains went up and others went down, ticks clicked, and many locks unlocked and the giant wooden bar running through the gate was removed. Next the guards all grabbed their part of the handle. All the while the Trocarians were marching with pride over their victory against the demarians.

Aloysius was in the lead, and he was overcome with joy. He did keep his cool; he didn't want to embarrass himself in front of his men. The Trocarians continued marching in unison.

"Open the gates!" yelled a guardsman on the top of the gate. Then the gate guards pulled on the handles with all their might. The gate slowly opened and the Trocarians marched through as the gate opened. They were still marching in unison.

Upon seeing Aloysius, Farah was overcome with joy and ran towards him. When the Trocarians marched to the state of the emperor, located in the heart of Sinsoria's first level, they were greeted by thousands of cheering peasants and citizens. Flower petals were falling like rain upon the Trocarians. When they reached the statue they all surrounded it and then took a knee. Aloysius stood in front of his army the cheering grew silent, Aloysius then proclaimed, "The emperor was with us today. Let us honor our fallen brethren and pray to once again face the demarians so that we may avenge our fallen brothers and aid the demarians to meet THEIR OBLIDERATION!!!" The Trocarians let out a cheer that shook the walls of nearby houses and rose to their feet.

Suddenly they fell silent again and took a knee once more. Aloysius was confused for a moment before he felt a powerful presence behind him. He turned to see Aaromir standing behind him. Aloysius felt humble,

"My lord," he knelt down, "we have claimed victory over the demarians. It has cost us 10,000 of our brethren, but we did come out victorious."

"I am glad of your victory. I'm also sad since 10,000 have died, but their deaths shall not be in vein. I am especially proud of you Aloysius,"

"Me sire?"

"Yes, you have done extremely well for your first battle. 10,000 dead, not a good total, but the other two leaders have come back with at least fifteen to twenty thousand dead. You have only 10,000 dead, it's not great, but it is pretty good for your first battle." Just then Farah came up to Aloysius and threw her arms around him. She began kissing him repeatedly from cheek to cheek. Aloysius began to blush.

"Mom!!!" moaned Aloysius, "not in front of my army!" Then he heard the Trocarians chuckling. Farah stopped then sighed joyfully, "Sorry."

"Your mother?" asked Aaromir.

"Yes my lord" replied Aloysius.

"Ah, she was worried sick about you."

"I can tell."

"Now that you have arrived, I guess it is too late to send you on a rescue mission."

"Rescue mission? Who? Where? Why haven't you told us sooner, if our brothers are in trouble than we can help them. Come Trocarians, our…"

"No Aloysius," interrupted Aaromir," your men must rest; if there's one thing I've learned in all my years as emperor it's this. If the men don't rest after every battle, than they won't be as able fighters and be nothing more than meat shields. Don't trouble yourself, I have already sent the knights to save our brothers at the Olditron Canyons."

"Very well my lord," replied Aloysius noble.

On the far reaches of Sinsoria lie the Olditron Canyons, large rock ways that narrow down into a pathway able to fit 100,00 men. Whoever controls this region can transport troops all across the western hemisphere of the planet and can also resupply forces rather quickly and can also transport supplies safely. The Sinsorians and demarians have been fighting over control of this region for many months now. However, the demarians are becoming increasingly desperate. They have been trying to gain some or any advantage over the Sinsorians for many centuries now. The Sinsorians somehow manage to take away all advantages and use them for their own gain.

Now however, was a golden opportunity for the demarians. Aaromir had dispatched an army of 300,000 Sinsorians to hold the pass. Due to many attacks and heavy fighting with the demarians, the number has been reduced to 100,000. The Sinsorians use to be able to successfully hold the pass. Their chances of successfully holding the pass are becoming slimmer and slimmer with each passing day as more and more men are dying. The Sinsorians at the canyon are in a desperate need for reinforcements. Aaromir is already aware of this situation and has sent many reinforcing armies in order to aid the Sinsorians that are trapped at the Olditron Canyons.

The demarians however, keep turning back the reinforcements and are denying aid to the Sinsorians at the Canyons. To make matters worse, the demarians have found a new general, and he is ruthless beyond reckoning. He is in command of the forces assaulting the Sinsorians at the pass. His name is Ramigious, and he has changed the barbaric demarians into an elite fighting force.

Ramigious is twice the size of the Sinsorians, as the rest of the demarians. He is also heavily armored, and wears a full faced knight helmet that covers his entire face except for an opening around the eyes. His shoulder plates have mini-spikes sticking out of them from all sides and wrap around the plate, covering it in spikes as if it is a large mace. His knees have horns that lunge outward and curve towards the sky. They are a foot high and a foot long. From his shoulders, three foot spikes extend out from his shoulders. The spikes are three feet in length and, like the knee spikes, curve upward and are three feet in height.

Ramigious was a military mastermind. He knew the best formations, tactics, and timing of attacks to take. This knowledge easily earned him the rank of general. Before Ramigious came in command, the demarians would throw everything they have at the Sinsorians in one big wave. This, of course, was a losing strategy which was used to the Sinsorians's advantage. Since the demarians would throw everything they have at one time, the Sinsorians began to move in vast numbers since they suffered many defeats the first time this strategy was tried. This way, when the demarians are defeated, the Sinsorians stand victorious and can live to fight another day.

Ramigious changed the demarian way of attack. Instead of hitting everything at once, Ramigious hit a little at a time in waves. Each wave would be stronger than the last, and each wave would weaken the Sinsorians so they would be unable to fight off the next wave. This new strategy has won the demarians many victories and dealt crushing blows to the Sinsorians.

Now this new strategy is being used at the Olditron Canyons against the Sinsorians. However, the Sinsorians are fast learners and can figure out ways to counter this new tactic. At the pass the Sinsorians have formed ranks, pike men wielding long spears have formed double lines with spears extended. The first line is kneeling down, while the second line is standing holding out their extended spears. Behind them are the musketeers, safely firing at the approaching demarians. They have formed into three firing lines. Their muskets are being fired from between the heads of the pike men in front of them. When the first line is given the command to fire, they fire then kneel down and begin reloading. Then the second line is given the order to fire, they fire, then also kneel down and begin reloading. After which the third line is given the order to fire.

By the time the third line kneels down and begins reloading, the first line is finished and they stand back up and fire, then the second and the third and the cycle keeps going. This constant barrage of fire mows down many charging demarian waves. Then the remaining demarians would run straight into the waiting line of spears. The Sinsorians were sure to line up from wall to wall, this way the demarians could not flank them and had run straight into them. When the demarians ran into the wall of spears, the sound of armor breaking and flesh tearing rung out. The demarians were stabbed in the waist and also in the chest. When a demarian ran into the wall, he would stop when the spear ripped into his waist.

However, the other demarian behind him would run into him, forcing him forward into the spear of the standing pike man and forcing the spear in his waist to go further into his body. Sometimes two demarians would get stuck to one spear. What's more is that the musketeers would still continue their barrage of fire, killing many demarians and finishing off injured ones. While the demarians would try and break through the lines of pike men, the swordsmen would flank them from both their right and left sides. The swordsmen would charge into the demarians flanks and begin killing them off.

As the swordsmen hammered through the flanks, the rear demarian units would be cut off from the forward units. When the demarians get separated, the pike men and musketeers begin pushing forward while the swordsmen hit the demarians from behind. When the forward unit is completely destroyed, the swordsmen regroup and charge the rear units while receiving fire support from the musketeers, who are firing from ledges about ten feet off the ground. The demarians would take many losses then realize that they are about to lose and retreat.

The Sinsorians would celebrate, but only for a short time. They would let out a small cheer, and then prepare for the next wave of demarians. The leader of the Sinsorians is one of the noblest and finest warriors. He is one of the few leaders who would lead Sinsoria's armies to victory in dark and hopeless moments. (He was a close friend to Ehandor, they fought many battles together). His name is Adrastros. He is one of the most intelligent military strategists in all of Sinsoria. It was Adrastros's idea to form the wall of pikes and place the musketeers where they were so they could provide fire support. It is the genius and sheer will of Adrastros that has helped the Sinsorians hold the pass for three months now and against five waves of demarian assaults.

Though supplies and munitions are able to reach the Sinsorians, they desperately require reinforcements. With every wave, more and more Sinsorians are being killed.

"How many men did we lose with this wave sergeant?" asked Adrastros.

"About 100 men sir." Replied the sergeant doubtedly.

"If we keep losing men like this, than I fear we shall lose this pass and with it, a critical advantage against the demarians." Adrastros denounced sadly. Then one messenger came and informed Adrastros that the knights had been dispatched and were on their way.

"Excellent, now all we have to do is just make sure that we're still alive when they arrive," proclaimed Adrastros.

Just then a Sinsorian cried: "My lord, sixth wave approaching and it looks like Ramigious is leading this assault. What do we do!!!?"

"Sinsorians!!!! My brothers, prepare for battle!!!" Then the Sinsorians all rushed to their positions. Adrastros had instructed the musketeers standing on the ledges to stay where they were. As the demarians marched closer and closer, the musketeers were all loading up their muskets and waiting for the command to fire, Adrastros made his way to the front of the army. He looked back and saw his men with scared expressions on their faces. He knew that it wasn't fear that gripped them, but anxiety. They were anxious for this final fight.

Just then the demarians began charging, the Sinsorians held their ground. As the demarians got closer and closer, the men began exhaling slowly. When the demarians were about 500 yards away, Adrastros began to lift his hand slowly.

"MUSKETEERS," he called out" On my command!" The musketeers then all lifted their muskets up into a firing position, and aimed at the demarians, who were coming ever so close. Adrastros waited patiently with his arm raised as the demarians charged closer. The musketeers held their finger as the trigger as they waited for the command to fire.

Adrastros watched on patiently. Then as the demarians ran faster and came closer, one of them stepped on a small boulder that was instantly crushed beneath his massive foot. As soon as Adrastros saw the crushed boulder, he yelled out "FIRE!" and threw his arm down. The second his hand came down, all the muskets went off simotanesly and the men were covered in a fog of smoke. When the muskets went off, 3,000 demarians went down smashing to the floor, 100 meters away from the men. Then Adrastros pulled out his mighty two-handed sword and urged "Come on men, fight for all your worth," (he then lifted his sword into the air), "FOR THE EMPEROR!!"

Then the men all let out a scream and ran out of the fog before it began to lighten. While the front of the demarian force had been destroyed, the middle and rear units had regrouped. This gave the men precious time and allowed them to gain far more ground. Seeing the Sinsorians closing in, Ramigious ordered the remainder of the first charge to attack. They took full speed at the Sinsorians.

As the two armies moved closer to one another, the musketeers began to reload their muskets. They had stayed behind in order to protect the pass in case the swordsmen and pike men were all killed. Just then the two armies collided. The Sinsorians, greatly outnumbering the demarians, had easily surrounded them. Before the armies had collided, Adrastros had swung his two-hand blade into the legs of a charging demarian. The blade sliced his legs off and caused him to fly forward and land on his face.

Adrastros then turned around and thrust his into the back of the demarian, killing him. Then Adrastros pulled out his sword, and turned around just in time to block an attack from a demarian. Adrastros held the blade with all his strength. Then he began pushing the blade upward, he then used his sword to turn the demarian blade and he forced it to the ground and pinned it there. All the while his sword was still held against the demarian blade.

The demarian tried to lift his sword but Adrastros was a little stronger and was able to hold the sword down. He couldn't lift it, even for a brief moment to strike, than that would leave his entire chest open, and the demarian would size that opportunity and thrust his sword into his chest. So Adrastros dared not to lift the blade. He then thought on his feet, Adrastros slammed himself into the demarians chest.

The blow knocked the demarian to the floor and caused him to drop his sword. Adrastros then lifted his sword handle above his head and thrust it down into the chest of the demarian. Adrastros pulled his blade out of the demarian and then the armies smashed into one another. Due to their superior number, the Sinsorians were able to fight the 20,000 demarians easily. Five men would fight one demarian at a time. This tactic allowed the men to easily kill off the demarians. Whenever one demarian swipes his sword, a Sinsorians would block it, and the other four would slice, lunge, stab, and slash their swords into him. Then move out of the way as he fell, and leave to help their brothers. Some demarians would be able to kill all five men and then move on to kill more before dying.

The pike men would thrust their long spears into the demarians and keep pushing it through until the demarians fell on their knees, and begin to fall sideways, and then they would pull out their spears. One pike man had his pike extended while he was charging. When his tip met with the stomach of a demarian, he jumped and forced the demarian down and the spear head further into him, killing him before he hit the floor. Another demarian was charging when a pike man lunged his spear into him. The demarian stopped as blood began to leak from his helmet. He then switched his mace into his right hand and grabbed the pike with his left.

Instead of trying to pull the pike out, the demarian thrust it further into him. He then took his hand off and grabbed the spear again; he thrust it even further into himself. He grabbed and thrusted three times before the pike man was within striking distance. The pike man was horrified and paralyzed with fear.

He was shaken out of this fear when the demarian had punched him. Then while he was still recuperating, the demarian brought back his left hand and again punched the pike man, but on his left cheek. The demarian again brought his hand back and punched the pike man on his right cheek, turning it red. He then punched the pike man on his left cheek, turning that red also. The pike man turned and spat out the blood in his mouth.

When he turned back to face the demarian, the demarian landed a punch right between the pike man's eyes. This broke his nose and caused him to let go of the pike and back away in pain. The demarian then grabbed the handle of the pike and broke it in two. The first part still lodged within him. Then the demarian held his mace in both hands and began to run at the dazed pike man. The pike man was screaming in pain as he tried to pop his nose back into place. When he did, he turned to see the demarian running at him.

He did not have time to react. When the demarian reached him, he swung his mace at the pike man's leg, knocking him to the floor. Then the demarian smashed his mace into the head of the pike man, hearing the sound of his skull cracking. Just then, three Sinsorians came from behind the demarian as he fell to his knees. The first one thrust his sword through the demarians back and forced it through until it came through his chest. Then the demarian jerked up in pain. The second Sinsorians sliced the demarian across his chest, which caused him to place his hands over his bleeding chest and shiver with pain.

The third and last Sinsorians thrust his sword in the neck of the demarian which caused his head to jerk sideways. When the Sinsorians pulled his sword out, it was painted red instead of silver. The lifeless carcass of the demarian then slumped forward and landed on top of the body of the pike man he had killed. The rest of the demarians were killed off easily and the men all regrouped.

Then Ramigious commanded the rest of the demarians to charge. Adrastros did the same with the men. When the armies collided, at first there was no push on either side. For every Sinsorians that was killed, a demarian fell as well. Then the Sinsorians began to push forward and more demarians began to fall.

"They're breaking, now is our chance men of Sinsoria!!!" roused Adrastros, "Forward!"

The men then let out a scream and pushed onward. The demarians began to retreat, but slowly.

Upon seeing his warriors retreating, Ramigious decided to take matters into his own hands. He stepped down from the ledge he was on and began walking towards Adrastros, since he has seen that he is clearly the leader. Sinsorians began charging towards Ramigious. He sliced one Sinsorians then lunged his sword into a second one, killing them both. Then he back punched a third one, knocking him down to the floor. Ramigious wasted no time and thrust his blade into the Sinsorians chest. He then pulled out his sword and stabbed it into a fourth Sinsorians. Then he kicked a fifth one to the ground and spun his blade around and thrust it into the Sinsorians's chest. He then began to pull it out when a sixth Sinsorians came charging at him. Ramigious sliced his blade upward and slashed the Sinsorians clear across his body. The cut started from his lower waist, and ran diagonal all the way to the top of his forehead.

The Sinsorians stood there gasping in pain when Ramigious punched him with the back of his hand and forced him to look to the left as his neck snapped. The Sinsorians died instantly and fell backward. Ramigious then continued to kill until he had reached fifty dead Sinsorians swordsman and pike man. When the demarians saw Ramigious killing the Sinsorians, they become more motivated and began pushing back. By the time the demarians began pushing back, Ramigious was only a few feet from Adrastros. He began walking towards him. A Sinsorians swordsman had seen Ramigious killing his brothers and now sees him walking Adrastros, he charged at Ramigious with sword out and shield in front of him. Adrastros had seen Ramigious in action and when he saw the swordsman charging, he yelled after him and told him to stop.

It was too late. The swordsman was headed for Ramigious and was about to strike. Ramigious just simply grabbed the swordsman by his head. He didn't even flinch. His eyes were focused on Adrastros. The swordsman began swinging blindly. Then Ramigious crushed the Sinsorians head in his massive hand that engulf his head. Adrastros could hear the skull crushing and see the blood raining down from Ramigious's hand that gripped the swordsman's head. Adrastros also watched as the limbs of the swordsman went lifeless and just dangled in the air.

Ramigious then threw the lifeless body aside, as if it were nothing. Adrastros lifted his sword and charged at Ramigious, screaming as he ran at him. Ramigious held his sword up and prepared for Adrastros. When Adrastros reached him they clashed swords. Every time Adrastros tried to attack, Ramigious would block it. It is as if he knew all of Adrastros's moves before he even made them. Then when Adrastros tried to slice Ramigious's head, Ramigious blocked the attack, and kicked Adrastros to the ground.

Ramigious then moved in front of Adrastros and stomped on his arm, breaking it under the force of his massive foot. He then lifted his sword, above his head, ready to strike it down. Suddenly there was rumbling. Adrastros looked around to see what was going on. He saw the entire fight stop and everyone looking around. He also saw most of his men dead on the ground. While he was looking at the ground, he seen the rocks beginning to vibrate and shake. After a while, it felt as if the entire ground was shaking and the rumbling grew louder.

"Earthquake?" asked one Sinsorians.

"No, Knights!!!" implied Adrastros.

Just then a knight showed up on the hill with the break of sunlight behind him. This knight was Borachius, leader of the knights of Sinsoria. Borachius wore silver armor and had an open faced helmet that had a face guard he could lift at anytime. His horse was heavily armored and had a head guard with holes that went over the eyes so that it may see. The horse, like Borachius, wore silver armor. Borachius had a mustache and a beard, and a purple feather hanging out of the top of his helmet. This symbolized that he was leader. All the other knights had a blue feather and were also as well armored as Borachius.

Borachius then pulled out his sword and hollered in a heroic voice "Knights!" Just then all the other knights came to his side and showed up behind him. Upon seeing the knights, half the demarians forgot about the Sinsorians and charged at the knights, Ramigious was one of them. When Borachius saw the demarians charging he lifted his sword and cried out "Knights of Sinsoria, FOR THE EMPEROR!!!" Then he pointed his sword forward at the demarians. The knights let out a cheer and began to gallop with Borachius in the lead.

Then as the demarians got closer, the knights began to charge, all 500,000 of them. Their number was so large it covered the entire hill and half the field. As the knights got closer to the demarians, they began to pick up speed and charge faster. The knights then soon collided with the demarians. The demarians were no match for the powerful knights. One demarian struck his sword at a knight and struck him off his horse. The demarian didn't last long since the other knights ran by and sliced him as they went by. The knights then soon separated the demarians and trapped them in the heart of their formation as they circled around and killed any demarian that was not within the circle. When Adrastros saw this, he smiled and let out a cheer. The Sinsorians quickly followed after him.

Adrastros was aided up by two swordsmen, who then helped pop his arm back into place. Adrastros let out a grunt of pain when he could feel his arm again. He then took up his sword and roused the men.

"Come on men, this is our chance, FOR EMPIRE AND EMPEROR!!!" The Sinsorians all let out a cheer and charged at the remaining 30,000 demarians. When the knights saw the men charging, they opened formation and allowed the men through. When the men began fighting the demarians, the knights would charge in groups of 25 and slice the demarians as they ran across the field to the other side.

This allowed the swordsmen and pike men to easily kill off the demarians. The Sinsorians and knights kept on killing the demarians until Ramigious was left standing. The men surrounded him and the knights moved in.

"Wait," instructed Adrastros, "I'll take him." The men and knights backed off giving Adrastros and Ramigious enough room to fight.

They then clashed swords, and again Ramigious blocked every attack. Then Adrastros tried to slice Ramigious's head again, Ramigious blocked it. Only this time, Adrastros elbowed Ramigious in his chest, causing him to let his guard down. Then, without hesitation, Adrastros went behind Ramigious and stabbed his back. Ramigious bent back in pain then fell forward. Right when he hit the ground, Sinsorians reinforcements arrived by the thousands and the other Sinsorians and knights let out a huge cheer.

Out of the 100,000 that charged into battle that day, 20,000 were musketeers, and only 30,000 pike men and swordsmen were standing. It was a day of sorrow, but it was an even greater day of victory. Adrastros was astonished by his victory. 50,000 Sinsorians was a decent price to pay in order to save millions of lives.

When Adrastros and his men made it back to Sinsoria, they were commended for their valiant service and were finally able to get some badly needed and well deserved rest. That night while the Sinsorians were resting their weary bones, it was a grim scene on the battle ground. Everywhere one looked, they would see dead bodies of Sinsorians and more dead bodies of demarians. The Sinsorians who now guarded the Canyon pass could find no survivors or any signs of life. They all gathered at the pass and felt safe in their numbers.

Suddenly there was a movement in the darkness. One of the bodies seemed to be moving. Then a large blade was struck into the ground. Large hands grasped the handle and a body was lifted from the dead. It was Ramigious. Apparently the stab to the back that Adrastros had delivered was not enough to kill this great general. Ramigious forced himself up and stood on his knees. He looked around the battle field and saw all of his army slaughtered and killed. He then looked up at the sky and let out a massive yell in anger. This yell scared all of the Sinsorians. They all got up and began searching the dead bodies. The yell also echoed throughout the Canyons. When Ramigious saw the approaching Sinsorians, he forced himself up and limped away before he was discovered and vanished into the darkness of the night.

CHAPTER 5

The Betrayal

AFTER THE VICTORY AT THE Olditron Canyons, the word spread quickly through out Sinsoria. The Sinsorians found themselves wining more and more battles and losing less often. Within one week, Aloysius was able to capture a demarian supply base and win three battles at critical locations. Adrastros had his share in victories as well. Within that same week, Adrastros held crucial points and dramatically loosened the demarian grip over the western lands.

It was as if the victory at the Canyons was the turning point of the war. As the week came to an end, this theory proved and became more and more true. The word spread quickly and the men began to look for a new hope. All the Sinsorians rushed to aid in any way they can.

"The Demarian spirit has broken", informed Aaromir to his leaders and commanders, "we must seize this golden opportunity before it is lost and use every advantage we can find. For I believe that this war might finally come to an end. Rally the men and spread the word," demanded Aaromir. The word spread quickly and all the men were roused and all wanted a chance to fight the demarians.

Everyone was filled with hope when they heard that the war might finally come to an end. Everyone except one, Spehachor. Instead of hope, Spehachor was filled with envy and anger. The news of Aloysius's victories made him furious. The man he blamed as the source of his fury and the focus of his hate was the emperor himself.

"It's all because of you Aaromir," he murmured to himself with an angry voice.

"It's all YOUR fault that nothing has gone right in my life. I'll show you."

He then assembled an army of 10,000 Sinsorians and marched northward, to the Demarian lands. This land was crawling with demarians and they defend this area in massive numbers. Aaromir has decided to leave this region alone since every army he sent to take the area, no matter how large the number, never returned. Spehachor believed that Aaromir will commend him yet if he takes the region. The army that Spehachor had assembled was a small force of Corics who had only completed the first part of their training. There are three parts of training a Sinsorians must complete: part one training in using a weapon, part two mentality, and part three moral and to fear no fear.

With only the first part of their training complete, the only thing these Corics are good for is being meat shields. They don't even stand a chance against the demarians, in their current state of training; they don't even stand a fraction of a chance. Plus they can't call for reinforcements since Spehachor had taken this force in secret and had neglected to inform anyone where they were headed.

So now, 10,000 men are marching straight towards their death, just so Spehachor can gain commandment for himself. Sadly enough, the men think that this just all part of their training. After a few hours of marching, the Sinsorians had reached the entrance of the northern lands and had begun to walk into the region. The men have no clue that a massive demarian horde is surrounding them and is now closing in on their position right this moment. The men continued marching, unaware of the ambush they were clearly walking into.

As the Corics continued marching, darkness began to creep in on them and fear slowly began to grip their hearts. They began to huddle together with Spehachor in the lead. The Corics huddled and moved closer together. They then started to look around nervously and moved closer together trying to find comfort in their number. They just couldn't shake the feeling that they were being followed and a heavy burden of eyes watching them. Even when the Corics turned to look and see if they were being followed and saw that no one was behind them, they couldn't help but feel a chill crawl up their spine.

As they watched the rocks and boulders and ledges for any sign of movement, a dense fog began to move in. As the men marched further, the fog grew denser and the Corics began finding it hard to see Spehachor, even though he was only five steps ahead of them. The Corics began breathing heavily and nervously. Then they soon began hearing rocks tumbling on the cliffs beside them. They looked but saw nothing for the fog was too heavy.

Then they began looking around nervously. Then one Coric stumbled on a stick and fell. When he grabbed it to confirm it was a stick, he was stunned at what he grabbed. In his hand, he held the remains of an arm that belonged to a dead Sinsorians. The Coric dropped the bones and let out grunts of fear. He then began to breathe heavily and faster. He wasn't alone however. As the Corics marched on, they saw the skeletal remains of Sinsorians still within their armor.

The armor had long, deep openings all over it. Then the skeletons began to show up impaled on rocks and pinned against walls. There was one body that was laying on a rock, extending over it, with a sword through the area where the heart was supposed to be. Another body had a pike lodged in its chest. The body was pinned to a wall with the bony hands still on the handle where the pike pierced the armor. Fear now fully gripped then men and none could retreat, for they were terrified of the thought of being lost in this god forsaken place.

The men soon walked into a large open area. Here, there were far more bodies and it was a much more horrific and grim scene. The Corics continued to march until they reached the center and Spehachor held up his hand, indicating for the men to stop. Spehachor listened carefully along with the Corics, all went silent.

Suddenly they heard footsteps approaching. They all turned to face the direction in which the noise came from. Then they heard more footsteps, this time from behind them. Then more footsteps from the right side, then the other left side. Soon footsteps were approaching all over.

"Where's it coming from?" stuttered a Coric.

"All over, all around us!" stuttered another Coric.

Then just as quickly as the footsteps mysteriously came, they vanished. The men were confused and petrified. They formed a defensive circle and grouped together and began looking around nervously. Spehachor looked around as well. As Spehachor looked around, a demarian appeared out of the fog. He walked forward until he was completely visible.

Just then a second demarian appeared, then a third next to the first one. Then a fourth appeared from out of the fog. Soon more and more demarians began to appear out of the fog. As Spehachor looked around, more demarians came out of the fog. The Corics soon found themselves surrounded and outnumbered. They could not retreat for all exits were cut off. The Corics held their ground and watched each other. Silence fell over the field. The Corics dared not to breathe.

Then suddenly Spehachor pulled out his blade and let out a scream. While he screamed he pointed his sword at the demarians. Then he charged at the demarians. The men soon charged after him at the demarians, screaming along the way. The Corics and demarians collided. While Spehachor was killing freely, the Corics were being slaughtered. As they charged at the demarians, they were busy thinking about whom to dedicate the fight to since Spehachor never told them. This was a fatal mistake.

Before the men had to clash swords with the demarians, they were knocked to the floor and stabbed. The demarians easily overpowered the Corics, whose minds were occupied over either dedicating the fight to the emperor or empire. One Coric slashed at a demarian trying to kill him. The demarian side stepped out of the way as the blade came down to his previous position. He then elbowed the Coric in the face, causing him to let his guard down and back away. The demarian immediately seized the advantage and sliced the Coric across his stomach. He then brought his sword back and stabbed it into the Coric's stomach and pulled it out as the Coric fell. Another swordsman was fighting a demarian and winning. He used his shield to knock a demarian warrior to the ground. As he lifted his sword to finish off the demarian, another demarian came from behind and lunged his sword through the Corics back.

As the sword came through his chest, it was tainted with blood. This caused the Coric to drop his sword and put his hand around the red sword. Just then, the demarian on the floor picked up his sword and lunged his sword into the Corics stomach and pierced it through the spine. The demarians pulled out their swords and the Coric fell dead.

A musketeer fired his musket at a demarian, aiming for his head. He missed due to the extreme shaking in his hands because of his fear. Another demarian then came from behind the musketeer and slashed his back. The musketeer dropped his musket and froze in pain. However the pain did not last long, for the demarian then stepped forward and elbowed the musketeer so hard in the face; he forced his head back and snapped his back. The musketeer was dead before he hit the ground.

Another musketeer fired at a demarian and hit his target. This was his first kill; it would also be his last. For a demarian came from behind the musketeer and placed his hand on his shoulder. The musketeer didn't have time to turn around, for the demarian then pierced his blade through the musketeers back and through his chest. The sword was stained with blood. The musketeer held his hands near the red blade, gasping in pain. The demarian then threw the body aside.

While his men were being ruthlessly slaughtered, Spehachor was killing at will. He would duck under a swipe then stab at the demarian and turn around to stab another. He was completely focused on the fight in front of him. He did not view the battle as a whole. This was a crucial thing that all leaders must have. This allows them to know when to retreat and when to push on. However, Spehachor only cared about his own personal gain. This would prove to be one fatal mistake.

As Spehachor killed more and more demarians, he was unaware that his army has been completely destroyed and the other demarians are now closing in around him. Spehachor stabbed a demarian in the stomach, then ducked under another slash and cut the head of the demarian who tried to cut him. Then Spehachor sliced the back leg of a demarian, forcing him to the ground.

Then Spehachor thrust his blade into the demarian's chest. When he rose he saw the demarians completely surrounding him. He lifted his sword ready to fight on; a demarian came from behind and back punched Spehachor in the back of the head. The blow was so strong it dazed Spehachor and made him fall to the ground.

When Spehachor tried getting up, a demarian came and placed his foot on Spehachor's chest and held him down. Then, Spehachor began to look around in fear. He then saw an injured Coric trying to crawl away in order to save himself. He was stopped short when a demarian sword pierced his back and forced him to the ground. As the Coric died, he reached out in Spehachor's direction.

Spehachor could see tears rolling down from the Coric's eyes and a sad look on his face. His arm extended all the way before it fell to the ground, never to rise again. The demarian then pulled out his sword out of the Coric's back with the tip a very red color. When Spehachor looked away, he saw a demarian approaching him. The demarian was holding a naked blade, and with every step he took, Spehachor could see dust flying around the demarian's massive foot. Then the demarian stopped in front of Spehachor. Spehachor looked into the helmet of the demarian and saw blackness. However, he could feel the demarian's eyes watching him through the eyeholes of the helmet.

Then the demarian placed both hands on the handle of his blade and lifted it slowly. The demarian lifted his blade handle high above his head, as far as his massive arms could go. When he was ready to force it down, Spehachor began pleading. "Wait…Wait…Wait." Then the demarian forced his blade down and Spehachor yelled "WAIT!!!" at the last possible moment. The demarian stopped and the tip of the sword was touching Spehachor's breast plate. The demarian just watched. He then lifted and tried to strike again, "Wait!!!" pleaded Spehachor, "Aaromir sent me here," he lied, "It was against my will. I tried to refuse but sent this army behind me; he wants to kill you all. I told him not to for you have done nothing to harm us am I right?" The demarians began looking at one another. "Also," implied Spehachor, "I told Aaromir that we should make an alliance with you to end all the fighting. You want to know what his reply was?" asked Spehachor, "It was 'An Alliance?! With those savages? I'd rather die than ever become friends with those animals."

The demarians then all began to tighten their grips on their weapons and grunt in anger.

"Doesn't that make you mad knowing that the emperor would rather want a quick death in a time of war, than to rather live in peace? Doesn't it bother you knowing that every day, more and more of your kind are dying and being slaughtered like cattle? I mean you use to have a huge empire and your numbers were vast and you use to be able to live in peace and harmony."

"Now Aaromir controls your lands, he slaughters your kind, and he takes away your food and supplies and homes and drove you into the mountains so that you can scratch a living off rocks." Then the demarian that had his foot on Spehachor took it off and backed away. When Spehachor was about to get up, the demarian in front of him stepped forward and placed his blade in front of Spehachor as if asking him,

"What are you getting at?" Then, as if Spehachor knew what the demarian was asking, he promised, "Aaromir has caused so much harm to your kind. You want revenge, well let me live and you shall have it, "he scoffed in a devise voice, "you want to kill Aaromir, then I can arrange that," (he got up on his feet), "from this day forward, I hereby pledge my eternal allegiance to the demarians," (he bows down), "for Aaromir has hurt me as well and I too seek revenge."

"Together we can achieve this common goal and put an end to Aaromir's reign of terror! Are you with me?!" The demarians then all let out a cheer and from that moment on, things were about to go from good to bad for the Sinsorians.

CHAPTER 6

The Demarian offensive

WITH THE UNKNOWN BETRAYAL OF Spehachor, the Sinsorians scouts continued to inform him and the other leaders of vulnerable areas beyond Sinsoria's walls. The scouts wore long green hooded capes, and had gloves that went on their right hands and left openings for their fingers. The scouts had sword sheaths placed on their right hips and carry muskets with them strapped on their backs. The scouts are experts at camouflage and travel in groups of fifteen to twenty scouts. They would report any demarian activities and movements to the leaders who would then decide whether to attack directly or wait and gather more information. They also inform the leaders of where the demarians are moving so they are able to decide where and when to attack the demarians.

However, when Spehachor returned to Sinsoria alone, he was immediately exposed. It just so happened that a watchman had seen Spehachor leaving with that army of 10,000 Corics through the postern gate on the western wall of the empire. (A postern gate is a mini gate that is built within the wall to allow troops to easily move out without letting in any enemy since it only opens outward). The watchman then immediately alerted the emperor, who walked out of the throne room just in time to see Spehachor marching. So when Spehachor returned without the army, Aaromir was furious.

These men had not completed their training and were suppose to be fresh recruits, with their complete training, and replace the battle weary soldiers and give them time to rest. However, with 10,000 Corics dead, 10,000 Sinsorians will not receive their much needed rest. For this reason, Aaromir stripped Spehachor of his title of second in command. He also sent word out so no army or group of soldiers will be taking orders from Spehachor.

As punishment, Spehachor was banished from the ring of commanders, never to return. Also Aaromir gave him the simple duty of being a lone rider (the lowest possible rank in the army). The only thing a lone rider could do is ride out, find a demarian army or settlement, and report back to Sinsoria. They were not allowed to thin the army out like the scouts, who were able to fight the demarians. The scouts are among the highest ranking personal since they were the finest. Aaromir also forced Spehachor to begin his scouting run in the morning and not return until he has found some demarian trace. This was done on a daily basis.

Aaromir was clueless of Spehachor's betrayal. Spehachor would use this run to his own advantage by reporting to the demarians where vulnerable Sinsorians camps and supply routes were. The demarians would then move out and attack these targets. Spehachor would then return into the empire to retrieve more information about weaknesses for the demarians. So everyday Spehachor would go out on his scouting run, and he would report vulnerabilities to the demarians. Who would then exploit these weaknesses by destroying them, and then Spehachor would return to Sinsoria to find more weaknesses.

Within a few months, the demarians were able to choke supplies into Sinsoria and begin starving the Sinsorians. They also were able to claim many victories over the Sinsorians and claim vulnerable areas and camps for themselves. The Sinsorians defeats began to outweigh their victories. The demarians had pushed the Sinsorians back and reclaimed much of the land they had lost. They're numbers then began to grow. Within a few more months, one area claimed by the demarians went from 300 warriors, to 3,000.

These victories would not have been possible without Spehachor's help. Now, instead of telling the demarians only about vulnerabilities, he was telling them everything about the Sinsorians. He was ratting out flanking paths, army sizes, where retreating armies are, where main armies are headed, and ambush positions, what lands are poorly defended, where to cut off reinforcements, and where training camps are located. The demarians exploited every possible weakness there was.

Due to their constant raids on weak points, the demarians were beginning to spread the Sinsorians thinly across the planet. Also due to their growing strength and number, the demarians began attacking stronger areas and forces under Sinsorian control. They also began succeeding in that as well and in about three years, were in control of most of Sinsoria's strongest bases and had killed some of her strongest forces. The hopes of the war finally coming to near end grew dim. The men and towns people began to lose hope.

In order to regain lost areas, retaliate against the demarians, and rekindle the flame of hope, Aaromir began sending defensive escorts with the supply lines and sending armies double their usual size to retake camps and training grounds. This tactic worked exactly the way Aaromir hoped, only for a while. The tactic allowed the Sinsorians to gain some of the land they lost. Due to the daily reports Spehachor would give to the demarians, they were soon able to counter this tactic and regain the land they had lost. Also by this time, the demarians had grown stronger than the Sinsorians and easily killed the defensive escorts and the massive armies. Aaromir began to fear that if the demarian numbers continued to grow, they will soon be able to launch an attack on Sinsoria itself. This he cannot allow.

So Aaromir held a secret council with all of the leaders and captains. He purposely did not invite Spehachor since he was no longer a leader. At the council Aaromir discussed the current situation.

"The demarians have somehow gained the upper hand in this war."

"Yes I agree, they have gained much of the land and lost none."

"Also their numbers seem to be growing. If this is not stopped then the demarians would have marshaled up an army massive enough to launch an assault on Sinsoria itself."

"This we cannot allow."

"How can we stop them? All our efforts are futile and they seem to know all our moves before we even make them." Yes, they seem to know where we are going and when is the best time to strike. We have not been able to gain any ground, and have lost most of the land. The men are beginning to become more and more discouraged with every passing day. I fear they will lose hope before their lives."

"I agree," noted Aaromir, "there must be a turncoat in our mist. There is no other explanation as to how the demarians have known our every move. The question is who?" asked Aaromir and began thinking to himself. It had been nearly half a decade since Spehachor's betrayal. Sinsoria is a massive empire that spans one quarter of the land, and her armies were in control of much of the rest of the land. So it took a long time for the demarians to actually pin the Sinsorians to a corner and cut off their food.

"Could be anyone, we have millions of men and women within Sinsoria. It could take years to find the traitor and by the time we do we would have lost Sinsoria."

"Spehachor." Aaromir thought aloud. Now since Aaromir is the emperor, he has many unique characteristics, one including the best memory in the entire empire. This is why he was able to remember Spehachor and his crime. Aaromir's memory is so outstanding that he is able to remember in perfect detail who was wearing what and what they said.

"Pardon my lord?"

"Doesn't it seem odd that when Spehachor returned from the north our losses began to increase?" (Very few of the leaders had noticed that and most others had no clue what Aaromir was talking about, they just nodded vigorously to keep from looking foolish and make it look like they know what's going on when they clearly have no idea.)

"Yes I have noticed that."

"I as well."

"I can't be certain, but I am sure he is the cause of this. Ever since Spehachor returned and began his scouting routs, the demarians have known all our tactics and base locations."

"So what do you want to do my lord Aaromir?"

"First things first, we must make sure it is Spehachor. Have two of our finest scouts follow him without being seen. If it is him, than I shall deal with him personally. If he is not, then we shall have to keep searching."

Aaromir then ended the council and told the leaders not to speak a word to anyone but themselves and keep it amongst themselves. Then Aaromir called upon the two greatest scouts in Sinsoria. A pair of twins who have never failed any scouting mission they have been assigned. Their names are Boro and Doro. Their camouflage is so extraordinary that someone could be staring right at them and have no clue that their there. So Aaromir ordered them to follow Spehachor everywhere he went without being detected. Boro and Doro accepted the mission and set off.

After hours of searching for Spehachor, they then spotted Spehachor near the leaders' cabin, eavesdropping by the door. Boro was on the roof of the house near the cabin, staring right at Spehachor. They had snuck up on him so quietly that Spehachor never heard them coming. Spehachor had a feeling he was being watched and looked around. He stared at the roof in front of him, right at Doro, and saw nothing. So he shrugged and continued eavesdropping, looking around to see no one was watching him. However, he had two pairs of eyes watching his every move. Doro, the one on the roof in front of Spehachor, wore his gray cape to blend in with the roof tops and was crouching very low. Boro and Doro were flashing hand signals at one another about what they heard and saw.

Then one of the leaders spoke about a massive army moving through the Olditron Canyons to out flank the demarians and take back the Asnecon fields which would give the men a huge advantage over the demarians since they would be able to box them in from both sides, one force from the front and one from behind, and move in. (This of course was all misinformation since the leaders knew Spehachor was listening in and the Olditron Canyons were still under Sinsorians control, but have recently been cut off from the forces stationed there). When Spehachor herd this news, he murmured to himself, "Well, we'll just see about that." He then turned and ran to the stables to begin his daily "scouting run". When he left, the scouts came out of hiding and as one followed closely behind Spehachor, Boro then dropped down and knocked on the door to let the leaders know that they can now discuss their real plan and that they have began following Spehachor.

The leaders then began to discuss their plan to take back the lands. Boro and Doro stayed close behind Spehachor's tail. Doro ran along the roof tops, while Boro followed on close behind on the ground. When Spehachor reached the stables, he immediately got on his horse and rode off. Boro then reached out and jumped on his horse and rode after Spehachor, being careful to leave distance between him and Spehachor. This way Spehachor cannot hear the gallops of the horse behind him. Doro, who followed on the rooftops, jumped into a space between two houses that were very close to the gate. He had his horse waiting there in case Spehachor tried to make a quick getaway.

When the guardsman at the gate saw Spehachor approaching, they opened the gate and gave notice to Doro that Spehachor was approaching. Doro waited until his brother passed before galloping since he was not sure how far behind Spehachor he should be. When Boro then passed by, Doro then kicked his horse and began to gallop. When both scouts ran through the gate, the guardsman closed the gate.

The twins were about 45 feet behind Spehachor. Though they cannot be heard, they were defiantly within sight if Spehachor was to look back. However, since no one ever followed Spehachor, he had no reason to look back. He kept his focus ahead of him instead of what was behind him. This was very helpful for Boro and Doro since they did not need to worry about being seen. They still did keep a safe distance, fearing that if they moved any closer, Spehachor would hear them and look back.

"Where do you think he's going?" called Boro to Doro.

"I don't know!" replied Doro.

They were careful not to raise their voices too loud, incase Spehachor would hear them. They continued to follow him until the grass turned to gravel and the horse's hooves were running on pebbles. The sky began to darken and jagged rocks began to appear. Spehachor continued on his intended path around the jagged rocks. The horses began to become scared and tried to rear away. Boro and Doro knew the precise reason why. This land was the homeland and heart of the demarian forces.

This is where the bulk of the demarian forces are located. Fresh demarian warriors are spat out every day from this accursed region. This land is the main reason as to why the war drags on. Aaromir has been trying to devise a way to take control of this land, cripple the demarian war machine, and bring an end to the war. However, there is always something preventing Aaromir's strategy for taking the land. Due to the rocky rugged terrain, a flanking attack by the knights would be impossible. The massive size of the mountains would make it impossible for the musketeers to fire down on the demarians. The mountains are also so close to one another that the only way into the demarian homeland is by a narrow path that is within the center between the mountains. This path is so narrow that only six Sinsorians can move through at a time and only two Trocarians can move through at a time. The men would be so cramped, that they would not be able to draw their weapons or be able to dodge attacks. So a frontal assault would be a suicide tactic. For these reasons, Aaromir had put aside all hopes of attacking the demarians at their hearts.

The demarians have chosen this land for these precise reasons. The Sinsorians disadvantages are the demarian advantages. Thousands of demarians defend the pass from above and from below. So when Spehachor entered through the pass that runs into the land, Boro and Doro immediately stopped and looked on in disbelief.

"He's mad!" cried out Boro.

"Demaria, what madness drove him in there?"

"I don't know, he probably has a death warrant."

"I'm not sure if we should still pursue."

"Neither am I, nevertheless must we be sure if it is him who is the traitor."

"Isn't this proof enough?"

"No, I'm afraid not."

Boro grunted and decided that his brother was right and dismounted from his horse.

"Be careful, remember Demaria is crawling with Demarians, so we must be careful and not attract any unnecessary attention or we can just consider ourselves dead men."

"Agreed."

Then the scouts took off on foot, being careful not to attract any attention to them. They approached stealthily and out of sight. The first thing they had to do was to get to higher ground where they can hide behind better cover and where their grey capes would blend in more. When they entered the passage of Demaria, they were instantly gripped by fear. They knew that this was a cursed place to be in. However, the thought that they had to push on for empire and emperor broke most of the fear that gripped them and began moving forward along the sides of the pathway watching each other's back. They found a good enough ledge to watch over Demaria where they will be able to look for Spehachor with ease.

So they began climbing the walls, being careful to avoid any loose rocks. Before they would pull themselves up, the scouts would push on a rock to make sure it is sturdy enough for them to pull themselves up. After hours of climbing, they were about 450 feet off the ground, and Doro had forgotten to check a rock before he pulled himself up, the rock came loose and fell, along with a few pebbles. Luckily they had anticipated this and were climbing in a one to one cover formation.

Meaning that Doro would stay ahead of his brother. In case there was a loose rock, Boro would catch them and make sure none fall. So when Doro pulled that rock loose, he immediately turned and managed to grab the big rock. However, he was unable to catch the pebbles and called out to Boro who was under him, "Catch them!"

Boro then immediately looked up and saw the pebbles fly over his head. He turned around and grabbed the pebbles with his left hand and held on with his right. They both let out a sigh of relief and placed the rocks on a stable ledge that was too small for them to stand on, but large enough to place the rocks. After which, the scouts continued climbing to the ledge. Right when they reached the top, two demarians had walked right under them on the ground. If the rocks had fallen, then the demarians would have noticed them and spotted the scouts climbing and would have alerted the entire land before the scouts would have reached the top. Luckily, the demarians had not yet been alerted. So the scouts continued moving on. The further they walked into Demaria, the more frightened they became. With each step they took deeper into the land, fear tightened its grip on their hearts. The thought of completing this mission for the emperor and empire was the only force that was strong enough to have them push on ward.

When they reached the ledge, they were able to view the entire landscape. Jagged rocks and mazes of endless valleys filled with razor sharp rocks stretched as far as the eye can see and further. To successfully invade this land would take a number beyond reckoning. A number so massive that it would have to be able to overcome the thousands of Demarians who defend it and still have enough men to occupy the entire region. A number that only existed in the dreams and imagination of the Sinsorians.

While on the ledge, the scouts looked everywhere in hopes of finding Spehachor.

“Find him yet?”

“No, not yet.”

Was the constant question and answer reply between the scouts for half an hour. Then suddenly Doro shouted: "Wait look!" (Pointing at Spehachor) There he is!" The scouts were overcome with joy. That joy soon turned into disbelief then anger when they saw Spehachor talking to the demarians.

"That traitor!" exclaimed Boro.

"Hold on now let's not jump to conclusions. First let's get a closer look and see what he's talking about."

The scouts climbed down from the ledge and made their way to where Spehachor was located. After much climbing and avoiding the many patrols, the scouts were finally close enough to listen in on Spehachor.

"That's right," Spehachor confessed gradually, "the Sinsorians are marching a huge force through the Olditron Canyons as we speak to out flank us," The scouts could not believe what they were hearing. "We need to strengthen our defenses at the Asnecon fields and halt this army there. Once we have done that we can move our forces through the Canyons and take the entire land for ourselves. When we have done that, we will be ready to launch our massive assault on Sinsoria itself, take the city, and put an end to the tyrant, Aaromir." The demarians broke into a cheer.

The scouts were frozen in fear in disbelief and fear.

"I think we got what we needed," whispered Boro to Doro, "let's get out of here!" Then Doro nodded and they both began to slowly back away. But unfortunately Boro had leaned a bit too close to the edge of the ledge he was hiding on. When he was backing off, he had knocked some rocks down and they rolled down the hill and had hit Spehachor on his leg. Spehachor looked down to see the cause of his pain and traced it back to where it came from and saw the scouts backing away. He pointed at them and yelled "INTRUDERS,

INTRUDERS!!!" The demarians immediately stopped cheering and looked at the scouts. "We're spotted! GO!!!" and both the scouts got up and fired their muskets at Spehachor, trying to kill him. However, they each shot a demarian in the head, killing them both.

Realizing they had missed their target and had no time to reload, they turned and ran for it. Spehachor realizing what had just happened ordered the demarians to pursue the scouts, "After them!!!" he yelled. The demarians all ran after the scouts who were now many yards away. While they were running, Boro and Doro were trying to reload their guns. (This was a skill that all scouts had to master for they did not know, nor could ever know, when they would be caught.)

Doro had reloaded his musket and turned around and fired into the growing army behind them. He managed to shoot a demarian in the head and forced him to tumble over and trip the other demarian behind him. This helped stall the army for only a little, but gave the scouts more precious seconds to get further from the demarians and closer to the entrance of the land. The demarians tried slowing down the scouts with anything and everything. Some were trying to flank them but the scouts were too fast and easily passed the area when the demarians emerge. Others, who were on the top layer, were throwing down rocks and massive boulders.

Boro and Doro jumped, ducked, ran past, slid under, and side stepped out of the way of all the rocks falling upon them. However, one demarian managed to get all the way around Boro and Doro and cut them off just before the entrance to Demaria. When Boro was about to reach the entrance the demarian emerged a few feet in front of him. Boro knew that he would not have time to fight the demarian one on one with the army getting ever so close.

The demarian drew his weapon ready for a fight. Boro kept on running until he was within the reach of the demarian blade. He then drew his blade and swiped it upward at an angle and cut the demarian clear across the chest. He then sliced the sword downward at an angle at the opposite side of his first strike creating an X on the demarians chest. Then he cut the demarian clear across the center of the X to form a star on the demarian's chest. Boro then finished off his opponent with a stab in the center of the blood star he created on the chest of the demarian who fell dead after Boro pulled his blade out. To form a star and to kill the demarian, took Boro only five seconds from his upward swipe to his stab.

When the demarian fell dead, Doro shot once again into the army, which had now quadrupled in size. Doro killed one last demarian before Boro put his fingers to his mouth and sent out a loud whistle to call the horses. The horses galloped and stopped at the entrance, waiting for their masters. Boro ran, grabbed the sash and leaped onto his horse. He then waited for his brother, who ran onto a rock and leaped onto his horse.

Then they both kicked their horses and galloped away right when the demarian army had arrived. Spehachor pushed the demarians aside and watched the scouts ride away into the horizon. He then let out a massive yell in anger, knowing that he has been discovered. The demarians all watched him as he began to throw a fit. Then he came to his senses and called for his horse.

He believed that there still may be enough time to stop the scouts before they delivered their message to Aaromir. So he immediately rode off believing that there would be enough time.

However, little did he know that while he was throwing his fit, Boro and Doro had already alerted the emperor of

Spehachor's betrayal. When Spehachor reached Sinsoria, the gates guards opened the gates, and Spehachor quickly dismounted off his horse then broke into a sprint and immediately stopped when he saw a wall in front of him. Not a wall of stone, but a wall of men. Swordsman had formed a line and stood shield by shield. Between the shields the swordsmen were the long pikes of the pike men who were kneeling down between the swordsmen. And just behind them were the musketeers taking aim at Spehachor.

This is a formation that has almost never failed the Sinsorians. Aaromir and the leaders all refer to it as the "Wall of Steel." This was a dreaded tactic against the demarians and a winning tactic for the Sinsorians. The musketeers would fire at all approaching demarians in massive barrages of musket fire, killing many. Then the remaining demarians would run straight into the straight into the waiting pike men and swordsman who would then finish them off. This tactic has brought many victories for the Sinsorians. It has also brought defeats as well.

Sometimes the number of enemies is too great and while the Wall can kill many, it often shatters and the Sinsorians are then slaughtered. So this is a win, lose tactic. But used at right times, and it can achieve many victories. The wall would often shatter due to flanking attacks. The Wall of Steel's sole purpose is to halt demarian charges and allow Sinsorians to push forward and break demarian lines.

It is only a straight line. Therefore, leaving it vulnerable to all flanking attacks and attacks from behind. The Sinsorians know of this major weakness and for that reason they always form the wall in areas that are completely devoid of flanking maneuvers. The only way past the wall is through it. So now Spehachor finds himself facing the wall and no way around it. He turned to run but found another wall formed up behind him. He turned and looked up at the roof tops and alley ways, they were filled with scouts. All weapons were pointed at him and he was completely surrounded.

Spehachor kept on looking around trying to find a way out, but all exits were blocked. Then Aaromir showed up behind the wall in front of Spehachor. Boro and Doro showed up next to him and took positions on the wall. They both aimed their muskets at him. Aaromir did not look happy. Spehachor was gripped with fear.

"So," began the emperor, "been paying visits to Demaria lately?" Right when Aaromir spoke those words, Spehachor knew he had been discovered.

"Been snitching to the demarians lately? Trying to make new friends maybe?!" Aaromir's voice was growing louder and was filling with rage.

"But..." began Spehachor,

"Betraying us have you?!" Aaromir was now infuriated; his voice was reaching its loudest.

"Well you see..." mumbled Spehachor,

"KILLING US HAVE YOU?!!!" the emperor was now yelling at a voice of immeasurable furry and volume. This was a voice no one in Sinsoria has ever heard before. The Sinsorians who were next to Aaromir began to feel scared, Boro and Doro took a step away from the furious emperor, who had his hands on his hips.

There are only a few things someone could do to infuriate the emperor. Aaromir is the forgiving kind and is slow to anger. Any insults would usually be put up with three or four times, depending on how his day is going. All the occupants of Sinsoria prefer to stay on the emperor's good side since the last incident 3,000 years ago.

One day a man decided to challenge the emperor's might and brought down a statue dedicated to the emperor, with a mob of protesters who also sought to challenge the emperor's might. This mob believed that Aaromir had been on the throne too long and was now abusing his power. After the statue was brought down, the entire mob was arrested and brought to trial before the emperor himself.

Aaromir tried to allow the mob a second chance but quickly changed his mind when they insulted him by calling him a tyrant and the leader of the mob spat in Aaromir's face. Aaromir then ordered for the entire mob to be publically executed. Half the mob was hanged; the other half was decapitated by Aaromir himself. While the rest of the mob was hanging, they were trying to change the mind of the people to rebel against Aaromir. They were quickly silenced when Aaromir ordered the musketeers to shoot the hanging mob.

After the incident, no one dared to even think or dream of ever revolting against the emperor. The execution of the mob sent a message throughout all of Sinsoria. And ever since then everyone has tried to stay on Aaromir's good side. Everyone except Spehachor, who had a family history of hating the emperor. Historians have said that Spehachor is the great, great, great, great, grandson of the leader of the revolt 3,000 years ago. When Spehachor heard what happened to his grandfather, an instant hatred was spurred and drove all of his actions that led to the betrayal and where he stands now, cowering in front of the emperor himself.

"Spehachor, you are hereby sentence to death. ARESEST HIM!" ordered Aaromir. The Sinsorians then moved into arrest Spehachor. Spehachor realizing what was happening pulled out his sword and stabbed as approaching Sinsorians.

He then turned to block an attack from a scout, and then punched him in the face. Another Sinsorians tried to tackle

Spehachor, but Spehachor side stepped out of the way and elbowed the Sinsorians on his back, knocking him down. Spehachor then turned and leaped over the Wall of Steel that was set up behind him and ran then hopped onto horse and began galloping towards the gate.

"STOP HIM!" ordered Aaromir. All the scouts and musketeers began firing at Spehachor. Scouts took to the roofs to try and snipe him down. Spehachor kept on moving and was too fast for the swordsmen and pike men to keep up with him. Musket balls hit the walls, doors, windows, ground, and all other places except Spehachor.

When he turned the corner and headed straight for the gate, a line of musketeers formed behind him and took aim. Meanwhile all the swordsmen and pike men pursuing him were alerting all other guards to stop Spehachor. One swordsman, who was in front of Spehachor, tried to stop him by swiping his sword at him. Spehachor blocked the attack and sliced the swordsman. The swordsman fell dead and Spehachor continued his "flight to freedom". The Sinsorians saw Spehachor approaching and ordered the gate guard to close the gate.

However, the remains of a supply convoy were coming through the gate, and the people of Sinsoria desperately needed those supplies. The convoy was also moving slowly through the gates. Therefore, the gate guards could not close the gates. They did, however, try to stop Spehachor from leaving. This came to no avail since he simply just ran through them. When Spehachor made it past the gates, the Sinsorians all gathered at the walls and watched him gallop into the horizon.

"Well there he goes, that traitor." Said Kenneth. A musketeer let out a grunt and kicked the wall and cried out,

“I had him, WHY didn’t I shoot?” Then Aaromir came and watched Spehachor ride off.

“Shall we send the knights after him my lord?” asked a swordsman to Aaromir.

“No,” answered Aaromir, “he has no power anymore. Let him go,” declared Aaromir.

“However, if he dares to come back, I want no hesitations or regrets. Kill him,” ordered Aaromir. Then he yelled after Spehachor, with his powerful voice, “SPEHACHOR, from this day forward you are here by banished from the empire of Sinsoria and you are a traitor in every sense of the word!!” Aaromir’s powerful voice rung throughout all of Sinsoria, and inside Spehachor’s head as he rode away into the setting sun.

CHAPTER 7

The Sinsorians counter offensive

WITH THE BANISHMENT OF SPEHACHOR, the demarians could no longer receive information about Sinsoria's weaknesses. They didn't seem to view this as a major problem since they now had the upper hand in the war. The demarians were in control of 30% of the land and were losing it before Spehachor's betrayal. After the betrayal, within six years the demarians controlled 70% of the land. The Sinsorians were left with a mere 30%. 25% of which was Sinsoria itself. Without counting Sinsoria and Demaria which made up large portions of the lands, the Sinsorians controlled 5% of the land while the demarians controlled 95% of it.

Now without the constant flow of weaknesses flowing to the demarians, Aaromir viewed this as a golden opportunity and was going to take full advantage of it. Aaromir's plan was to launch a massive land offensive to retake the land. When he presented his plan to his leaders, their reply was simple:

"My lord, with what?"

Then Aaromir realized that he had overlooked the one critical fact, the men, and empire, were shadows of their old selves six years earlier. Sinsoria had nothing to strike back with. Ever since Spehachor's betrayal, Sinsorians numbers had dropped significantly. Their numbers were now a third of what they were. The Sinsorians use to outnumber the demarians 5 to 1. Now they outnumber them 3 to 1.

To make matters worse, the men lacked the strength to fight the demarians. Both body and spirit wise. The lack of supplies such as food, water, and medicine, has had devastating effects on Sinsoria. The entire eastern side of the empire was completely devoted of all life. The few survivors in the center and western side of the empire are now scraping for whatever crumbs they can find. The lack of supplies has also had its effects on the Trocarians as well. They use to outnumber the demarians 3 to 1. Now their numbers match 1 to 1. However, the demarians have the upper hand in the fight. Since there is hardly any food, the Trocarians cannot keep up their tremendous strength. And since they cannot keep up their strength, they can hardly lift their own weapons.

Sinsoria's elite offensive and defensive unit was now nothing more than big meat shields. The famine of food hit the knights hard. Their numbers fell from 500,000 to 100,000. The force that could once shake the ground with its march could now hardly cause a vibration. On top of it all, the men, women, children, and Trocarians of Sinsoria, were all hopeless. Hopeless of ever winning the war, hopeless of ever ending the war, hopeless of finding a reason to fight on any more. Because of one man's selfishness and fuel of vengeance, an entire empire was brought to its knees.

Aaromir's list of crisis and obstacles stopping his plans was made even worse with hopeless men defending the empires boundaries. With Sinsoria's enemy besieging it from the outside, and radicals striking at it from within, it now struggles to survive. These radicals were not making things any easier for Aaromir's situation. These radicals were criticizing the war and Aaromir's part in it. They said that it is his fault that they're in this dire state.

They criticized Aaromir's entire war effort and his promise to end it quickly. They said that it was his fault the war is still dragging on and that they could do a better job of ending it. Of course the Sinsorians didn't believe any of this radical talk since they knew well enough that Aaromir is doing everything in his power to end the war and bring relief to all. However, the Sinsorians did know that the war drags on because the demarians want it to drag on. They will not stop until all Sinsorians are killed. Then again, the Sinsorians's situation was desperate. Their main intension was to simply survive and help their families survive. Therefore, they were open to any ideas of quick relief and aid.

It's not that they didn't believe in Aaromir or want to betray him in any way. They knew that he was fully capable of fixing this tough situation and making everything all better if they just gave him time. Some were willing wait if it meant keeping their loyalty to the emperor. Sadly however, some could not wait and although they had full faith in Aaromir, their problems were getting worse every day and they just simply could not wait. The radicals promised immediate relief and a quick end to this war. They gained support, but not as much as they hoped. None dared to go against the faith of the emperor.

With each passing day, more and more Sinsorians were dying of starvation and more and more support was gained by the radicals. If they had about 10% of the population supporting them, one of the radicals could challenge the might of the emperor and run against Aaromir for the position on the throne of Sinsoria. With enough support, they could possibly overthrow the emperor. However, for the three months the radicals have been in Sinsoria, they have only gained 3% of support for their ideas from people who had been starving and suffering for six years. And the number of support the radicals were getting was slowly on the rise. Aaromir did have knowledge of this and decided that he had to act fast since time was running out. Aaromir was now willing to gamble since frontal assaults to retake supply centers would fail. This would add on to the mountain of failures and wipe away the pebble of victories.

Since Aaromir was gambling, he was thinking rationally.

"Since all our frontal supply lines have been cut off," he proclaimed, "why don't we send our supplies from behind?" He pointed out a secret mountain pass that he and his leaders know about. (Luckily, this pass was not told to Spehachor. So he and all of the demarians were clueless about it). This pass is incredibly dangerous and risky to take since it leads all throughout the Achricon Mountains and over three large demarian bases. And if the Sinsorians are not careful, then the demarians will discover them and the pass and use it to strike at the heart of Sinsoria from behind. This pass was originally supposed to be used for troop transport since it was a dangerous path to take. The path itself is 500 feet off the ground and one wrong step can cause you to fall to your doom. Dangerous the path may be, Sinsoria's crisis is deepening with each passing day, so all the leaders agreed to it without hesitation or opposition.

Boro and Doro were dispatched to lead an army of 50,000 through the mountain pass to safely guide the supply convoys through the path and to the waiting arms of the people. Aaromir told the men to fill their empty stomachs first when they reach the end of the pass. When they reached the end of the pass, it only took them a day of constant travel. The pass split up to the east and west farm towns and supply centers of Sinsoria. These centers were under the ever watchful eyes of the tower guards of Sinsoria. If any demarians force dared to come near them, all of Sinsoria would be alerted and a massive Sinsorian force would be sent out before the demarians could even have a chance to prepare for battle. Therefore, for this reason, the demarians stayed clear of both supply centers. This played perfectly towards the Sinsorians advantage.

These supply centers were the jewels of Sinsoria's supply infrastructure. They played a key role in nourishing and feeding all of Sinsoria's warriors and supporting all other supply centers. This is why their supply convoys were hit the hardest and were the largest. Their land has the purest soil of the entire planet. They have an abundant harvest all year round. Once Boro and Doro reached the supply centers and told them about the mountain pass, they began sending all their supplies from behind and cut off all frontal supply lines. (This did not cause the demarians to arouse suspicion since the centers had stopped sending frontal supplies for three months at a time and were about to try again. To the demarians, they thought that the supply centers finally got the message and realized that they couldn't send supplies forward any more).

The army of 50,000 Sinsorians filled and ate until their hearts content. They were overjoyed to be able to taste food again and once they were full they guided the convoys safely through the pass and made sure the demarians remained clueless of what was going on. They even made sure to be extra careful when they passed over the demarian bases. The journey back to Sinsoria took half of the day since the Sinsorians now knew where to go and how to get there and when the first of the supplies arrived, the Sinsorians let out a massive cheer and flooded the streets to fill their empty starving bellies. The people were about to attack the convoys when one of the leaders of the convoys stopped them and said:

"Take it easy everybody! No need to push or shove there is plenty for ever one and everybody will get their turn, I can promise you." And he pointed to the other convoys that were arriving in boatloads. The supplies arrived twice a day every other day. The supply centers took turns delivering the supplies to the starving people of Sinsoria.

As the constant train of supplies poured into Sinsoria twice a day every other day, this was possible since the supply centers had overproduction of their crops due to the many days they had not delivered, the Sinsorians numbers began to swell again. The army of 50,000 was now 70,000. The eastern side of Sinsoria began to fill with life again. The men began to regain their strength and hope. The Trocarian numbers were beginning rise again and their strength returned as well. They were now able to raise their weapons high above their heads and keep them there.

The knight's numbers rose as well. They went from 100,000 to 600,000, a force much larger than before. They regained their ability to shake the ground with their gallop. However, with all this joy came misery. When the first supply convoy entered Sinsoria, it all went downhill from there for the radicals. They came so dangerously close to opposing the emperor's might, at 9% of the 10% needed to run against Aaromir for the seat on the throne.

When the supplies reached the Sinsorians, the support for the radicals went from 9% to zero in an instant. The radicals lost all support and their hopes and dreams of being crowned the next emperor. For doubting the emperor's power and seeking to oppose it, all the radicals were executed for their treason. All those who supported their ideas begged for forgiveness from Aaromir. Aaromir easily forgave them since he fully understood their dire situation. But in order for him not to look like a pushover, all the people who had supported the radicals had to spend one month in prison for their treason. The people thought that was fair. Aaromir also made sure that the families of those who supported the radicals received the most supplies.

This showed all of Sinsoria that the emperor was a man who would easily let bygones be bygones and be a disciplined leader who doesn't always show restraint and gives appropriate punishments for the crimes committed. He was the understandable type and was a strong leader, and that is why all the people love him so much. He is the only one who truly cares about their problems individually and not generally, (which is what all the other four emperors before Aaromir did). And he did not let that stop his judgment on the punishment that should be given for the acts of treason anyone has done. No matter how well Aaromir knows them or their situation.

With Sinsorians strength returning and the population beginning to swell again, hope began to show in the faces of the people. Before the supplies had reached Sinsoria, Sinsorians numbers plummeted from outnumbering the demarians 5 to 1, to outnumbering them by 3:1. Trocarian numbers also dropped as well. They fell from outnumbering by 3:1 to evenly matching them 1:1. The drop in numbers for Trocarians and Sinsorians alike happened over the six year period.

Now it's a different story. In about a year, Sinsorians numbers skyrocketed and now they are slightly larger than what they use to be before the betrayal. However, they still outnumber the demarians 5:1. Trocarian numbers also rose as well. This time a full person greater than what their numbers were. Now the Trocarians outnumber the demarians 4:1. What's more is that the demarians are clueless of this spike in population and supplies reaching Sinsoria. They still believe that the Sinsorians are starving and are still dying out.

This gave Aaromir an idea. He decided to use this belief to his advantage. Sinsoria's strength was returning but she was still too weak to fight on. So Aaromir decided to keep the demarians thinking that the Sinsorians are still too weak to fight. This way they will have surprise on their side when they once again take the fields. So Aaromir decided to wait three years before going to battle again. He wanted the men to rest and gather their strength so when they do return to fight they're enemy, they will be stronger than ever before. So that's what the Sinsorians and Trocarians did. They waited for three years, silently gathering up their strength and waiting for the moment to attack. Aaromir's plan was to make the demarians weary from waiting and then hit them with fresh troops and retake the lands. And while Sinsoria's armies waited patiently, Aaromir and his leaders would devise a plan together to retake the lands and push all the way to Demaria.

It would take the supply centers and entire year to stabilize they're supplies and get them back to normal again. When that happened, they were able to continue sending supplies into Sinsoria using the Achricon Mountain pass in a more orderly fashion rather than trying to rush many things on the pass at once. The growing Sinsorians numbers helped greatly in stabilizing the supplies. The supply centers had more than enough supplies for the growing population and Aaromir didn't have to worry about a supply shortage anytime soon. This helped greatly in easing the burden off his shoulders and allowed him to focus more on his battle plans.

With two years remaining until the Sinsorians are able to reveal themselves to the unsuspecting demarians, the Sinsorians decided to use the free time they had to retrain themselves and receive better armor and swords to use against their enemy. Some Sinsorians decided to use the free time to spend some time with their families since they hardly get a chance to do so. Most Sinsorians spent the time resting and gathering up their strength. During the three year waiting period, the Sinsorians actually had the opportunity to get acquainted with one another and get to know the others family. Life for the soldiers was terrific. No worries, no need to fear, just sit back, relax, and spend the time with either your family or training.

While the soldiers were enjoying themselves and they're time away from all the fighting, Aaromir was finalizing his battle plans to retake the lands. The plan involved a lot of three prong attacks all over the demarian lines from all fronts. His plan was to use a combination of steady streamed small attacks and then hitting hard with one large force. These small attacks would take place one after the other during different times at different locations all across the demarians lines.

The whole point of these small attacks was to distract the demarians and cause them to spread their forces this in some areas. Once that is done, Aaromir would send a massive attack across the demarian lines from the front, pushing them back. This plan was put into action after the three years of relaxation were over. The three year period was the first real taste of peace the Sinsorians ever got and they enjoyed every second of it. They're only regret was that it wasn't going to last very long unless they end the war.

After the second year past, something gripped the men. With the day of the offensive approaching, the men found that they weren't able to shake the feeling of wanting to fight again. Everything they lifted, they used it as a weapon and pretended to fight. The women and children couldn't shake a feeling as well. Although they were glad to see their husbands and fathers again and spend some real quality time with them, they weren't use to having the soldiers home so long. The simple explanation was:

"Well five millenniums of war could have strange effects once all the fighting stops for a while."

With each passing day, the anxiety of fighting grew in the hearts of the people. Aaromir was glad it did. He joked around by saying:

"Great, now I don't have to worry about inspiring the men."

Some Sinsorians begged the emperor to let them out early since they were so eager to fight again. Aaromir knew their feeling since he did miss ordering the men out to attack and defend key areas. But, he told them to wait since the element of surprise was still building up as the strength of the people.

The Trocarians were even more restless. They began breaking and snapping all the furniture they could get their hands on. Aaromir was happy about this as well. For he now knew that the men will have greater moral in battle since they're so eager for a fight. Aaromir himself wanted to send the men into battle just to shut them up. However, Aaromir was a precautious and patient man. He didn't make a move until he was absolutely sure it was safe to move on.

During the first year of the three year waiting period, the emperor dispatched all of the scouts to examine the demarian lines. They all reported back saying that the lines were thick and almost impossible to break through head on. So Aaromir decided to wait and see if the lines were flexible and expendable. He dispatched the scouts again just a few days before the Sinsorians unraveled their little surprise. Just as Aaromir hoped, the scouts reported the lines to be thinner and that a frontal assault would be the best idea. By this time, the Sinsorians were completely restless and couldn't wait any longer. Their anxiety played perfectly into Aaromir's plan.

With the three years finally over, it was now time to put Aaromir's plan into effect. He first sent out the scouts to pinpoint the weakest areas of the demarian lines. They said that it was the left flank and it consisted of 50,000 demarian warriors. Aaromir dispatched an army of 200,000 Sinsorians. The Sinsorians completely obliterated the demarians and recaptured a vital supply post, thus opening up a pathway for supplies to enter Sinsoria safely from the front for the first time in nine years. When the demarians heard of this defeat, they didn't take it too seriously. They thought that it was Aaromir's desperate attempt to break the demarian hold of Sinsoria's supply lines. So they took 30,000 demarians from their center lines and attacked the Sinsorians (believing that they must have been completely worn out from that first attack. Still clueless of the secret supplies reaching Sinsoria from behind). This force of 30,000 was completely destroyed by the Sinsorians army.

Aaromir then sent a force of 300,000 Sinsorians and tore up the demarian right flank, opening up a road to safely transport troops. Again the demarians didn't take this too seriously since they still believed that the Sinsorians were ready to break. Aaromir was about to prove them dead wrong. He sent an army of 100,000 Trocarians and hit the demarians all across their front lines. The Trocarians completely crushed the demarians and forced them to retreat. Aaromir's plan was to attack in large forces not only to crush the demarian's spirit, but also to give all the men a chance to fight and get rid of their anxiety.

Now, the demarians began to see retaliation. However, they didn't view it as a major problem. So in order to "crush" Sinsorians spirit, the demarians pulled soldiers from their center right flank and reinforced their left flank. They thought that the Sinsorians would use the same tactic and that they would stop them and regain the land they lost. However, Aaromir knows better than to use the same tactic twice.

This time, Aaromir sent out an army of 30,000 Trocarians and completely wiped the floor with the right flank. Alarmed, the demarians moved even more units from their center and some units from the left flank and tried to retake their right flank. They failed miserably. Aaromir then dispatched the knights to attack the left flank. They tore right through it. The emperor never gave the demarians time to recuperate. He sent out an army of 500,000 Sinsorians and they easily smashed through the thin lines and, again, forced the demarians to retreat.

The demarians now realized that this was not an act of desperation, but a full on retaliation. Even though they have lost thousands of soldiers and quite a bit of land, they still haven't given the Sinsorians attacks the attention they should be given. They still believed that they could turn back the advancing Sinsorians and Trocarian armies. So what they did is pull warriors from the rear and place them in front. This fortified the front but severely weakened the rear. This left their back completely vulnerable to attacks from behind. The flanks and the entire front were heavily fortified with troops.

Aaromir knew that the rear was completely exposed. He exploited this weakness by having the knights attack and push in from behind while the Trocarians push in from the front. This tactic couldn't have worked any more perfectly. The knights and Trocarians tore the lines apart and regained a massive amount of land. This is because the demarians had moved units from the lands to the rear in order to strengthen the fronts. When the fronts were torn apart, there was no resistance to stop the Sinsorians.

Aaromir's plan was working better than expected. His men kept on hitting demarians lines from all over constantly pushed them back and regaining the land. The Sinsorians pushed the demarians further back with every passing day. Within six months, the Sinsorians had pushed the demarians back so far and regained so much land that the land claim was now split 50% Sinsorians and 50% demarians. Now, the demarians were dead focused on stopping the Sinsorians. They reinforced their lines on all fronts. They weren't halting the Sinsorian advance, but they were slowing them down dramatically.

The Sinsorians and Trocarians were meeting with heavy resistance on all fronts. Though they were advancing, they were moving extremely slowly. Aaromir knew this as well. He spent most of his time trying to figure out how to make that final push into demarian lands since they had already reclaimed all the land they had lost. Now, Sinsoria's population had doubled. Supplies and fresh recruits were pouring into the empire at a constant rate. All supply lines were reconnected and reinforced. The Sinsorians established a massive number of military bases all across the land. With the constant flow of supplies and recruits, there was no shortage of eager fighters.

The most troubling thing of all was finding out a way to break the demarian lines. Aaromir and his leaders spent days pondering over a plan. The demarian lines were too strong and are holding all frontal and flanking attacks back. The plan finally came when Aaromir had summoned his leaders to a meeting to discuss their battle plan. It was suggested by one of the leaders who was in the leader's cabin before Spehachor's banishment.

Oddly enough, it was the fake plan that was only spoken to weed Spehachor out. At first, everyone opposed it. When the leader explained the current situation and how they would have the element of surprise, everyone seemed to like the idea.

"I like it, I like it, sounds like a plan," complemented Aaromir, "however, if we are going through with this, then I'm going to have to add a twist to it."

So the emperor sent Boro and Doro to the Olditron Canyons to search for any sign of demarian activity. Sure enough, there was an army of 150,000 demarians guarding the rear of the Olditron Canyons and the Asnecon fields. Boro and Doro immediately went back and reported what they saw to the emperor, who instantly dispatched an army. Turns out that the demarians still believed an army was coming through the Olditron Canyons. An army did emerge from the Canyons, but not what they were expecting.

While the demarians waited patiently watching the Canyon exit, they heard a noise. It was faint, but it grew louder as it got closer. The closer and closer the noise got the more familiar it sounded. It sounded like an army was approaching. The sound of heavy metal clanking echoed throughout the Canyon as the army drew nearer. The demarians readied their weapons. They drew their swords from their sheaths and held them in both hands, waiting for the army.

Suddenly, Aloysius appeared in the Canyon door way, holding his halberd in both hands. Then a Trocarian appeared behind him. Then another, and another, and another, soon an army of 50,000 Trocarians marching in perfect unison, footstep for footstep, appeared behind Aloysius. The demarians flinched a little but held their ground. Then Aloysius yelled:

"Trocarians, FOR THE EMPEROR!" and began charging. The Trocarians let out a scream then charged straight into the demarians. Aloysius swung his halberd into the chest of a demarian and forced him into the ground killing him. He then ducked under a sword swipe by a demarian warrior and picked up his halberd and swung it into the neck area of the warrior, slicing off head.

The Trocarians were hitting the demarians with everything they've got. Some are bashing them with their shields, others are ripping them apart with their swords, and it was just an all out massacre. Some Trocarians began pushing through the demarians. However, due to their number, they could only go so far. The demarians began to push back since they outnumbered the Trocarians.

Just then a voice let out: "FOR THE EMPIRE!!" and Sinsorians let out a scream and charged. Aloysius hacked a demarian in his chest then turned to see Adrastros's men charging with him leading them. The swordsmen and pike men smashed into the demarian right flank. Upon seeing this, the Trocarians pushed forward. They carved a path through the demarians straight to the Sinsorians. The musketeers were completely obliterating the demarian warriors.

They fired in barrages killing 20 demarians every time. With the combined force of 40,000 Trocarians and 300,000 Sinsorians, Adrastros and Aloysius worked together to encircle the losing demarians. Once Adrastros seen that the demarians were beginning to retreat, he ordered the musketeers to fire at the demarians rear units. The musketeers unleashed a massive barrage of musket fire into the demarians and killed 3,000 retreating units. Then Adrastros ordered 5,000 pike men and 5,000 musketeers to move around back and cut off the demarian retreat.

The pike men formed their spear wall where half kneel and the other half stand with pikes extended. The musketeers did what they did at the Olditron Canyon pass. They formed into three lines and unleashed a barrage of musket fire. The demarians charged into the wall of pikes and muskets in hope of breaking it. The demarians were all killed. What was left of the demarian army of 150,000 was surrounded on three sides and taking heavy casualties.

After two hours of heavy fighting, the army of 150,000 was now 90,000. However, they still fought on. They began to push back when suddenly a cry wrung out: “FOR THE EMPEROR!!” shouted a voice, and then followed by the neighing or horses and the sound of horse shoes running and smashing against the floor. It was the knights of Sinsoria led by Borachius. There were only 30,000 of them and they charged into the demarian left flank. Now the demarians were surrounded on all sides and had no way of retreating.

The only option they had was to fight until the last man standing. So they fought on. Badly outnumbered and completely surrounded, they all fell quickly. The pike men would impale one or two demarians while the musketeers fired massive barrages into the army. Within three hours, the fighting was done and the Sinsorians all remained victorious. Out of the 50,000 Trocarians that charged into battle, 30,000 remained standing. Out of the 300,000 Sinsorians that charged into battle, 210,000 remained standing. Out of the 30,000 knights that charged into battle, 25,000 remained standing. This was a tremendous victory and these lives were a small price to pay for it. The original plan was to send an army through the Olditron Canyons to take the Asnecon fields and hit the demarians from the rear.

Since the whole point of this plan was to throw the demarians off track and expose Spehachor, there were a huge number of things that could be done differently. This is the "twists" Aaromir was talking about. First, Aaromir sent an army through the Olditron Canyons and play into the demarian's "trap". They believed he would send an army of Sinsorians, not Trocarians. Second, he sent Adrastros from the entrance of the Olditron Canyons straight towards the demarians to hit their right flank. Lastly, he sent the knights through the Olditron Canyons and had them come out on the far exit, (this is why it took them so long to join the fighting). They then charged into the demarian left flank and once all armies were together, they engulfed the demarians and completely wiped them all out before they had a chance to alert the other forces.

Now the Sinsorians have an open passage straight behind demarian forces. Aaromir will use this pass to move behind the demarian forces and hit them from behind as well as in the front and allow his troops to move further into demarian lands.

CHAPTER 8

The final push

WITH THE SINSORIANS IN CONTROL of the Asnecon fields and the Olditron Canyons, Aaromir's tactics grew harsher. Now the Sinsorians were able to outflank the Demarians and hit them from behind across all fronts. Aaromir sent waves and waves of thousands of Sinsorians through the fields. The Demarians were taken by complete surprise. Their lines were torn to shreds and they were forced back.

Aaromir had the Sinsorians all across the front lines fall back and replaced them with Trocarians. All the Sinsorians were directed through the canyons and were ordered to move through the fields. With the Trocarians moving in from the front and the Sinsorians pushing in from behind, the Demarian lines broke and snapped like twigs. The Sinsorians pushed further and further into Demarian controlled lands. The further in the Sinsorians went, the heavier resistance they encountered. The Demarians tried to regroup their lines into a half circle to cover their flanks and prevent attacks from the rear. This was an act of desperation to at least slow down the advancing Sinsorians. This act was a complete failure.

When the Demarians pulled back to regroup, so did the Sinsorians. Spearheaded by the mighty Trocarian armies, they attacked the Demarian center. With the combined strength of both Sinsorians and Trocarians, the Demarian formation fell apart. The Trocarians alone dented the demarian lines. With the support of their Sinsorian brethren, the Trocarians broke the half circle and turned it into a "U".

Once the formation was broken, the Sinsorians and Trocarians spread out in all directions. The Demarian formation was torn apart from the inside out. Those who were lucky to escape joined the rear units of Demarians to help defend their borders. The land difference was 50% to 50%. Now it was 65% to 45%, the Demarians being the 45%. The Demarians now doubled defenses on all forces across all fronts, desperate to defend their land claims. The Sinsorians and Trocarian lines reformed and attacked the Demarian lines.

After two years of hammering at one another, the Demarian lines finally held and the Sinsorian advance had been stopped in its track. Seeing the Demarian lines repel all attacks from all sides, Aaromir called his leaders for a meeting to decide their next plan of attack.

"As well as you all know," began Aaromir, "the enemy lines are holding on all fronts. There seems to be no dent in their lines. So I'm open to any ideas."

“Well we can’t just blindly throw troops at them,” proclaimed one of the leaders, “we need a plan of attack since we are getting nowhere with what we’re doing now.”

“I agree,” said Aaromir, “although we’re inflicting major casualties to their lines, the Demarians are replacing and reinforcing their lines with fresh recruits. Therefore, preventing any advance by any of our forces.”

“Well my lord, since the Asnecon Fields and the Olditron Canyons are in our control, we can reinforce our frontlines easily. However, with the constant supply and reinforcing of fresh troops to both sides, I fear the fighting will continue to go on and cost millions of lives.” expressed Adrastros. (Aloysius was leading the Trocarians on the front lines hence his absence from the meeting).

“Whether we can reinforce our men or not is not what’s concerning me. What really worries me is the troops themselves.”

“My lord?”

“If the men continue to fight and not advance, I fear it will have a devastating effect on moral. The men will lose all hope and will to fight and just give up since they would see no point of fighting a never ending battle. All that we have been working so hard for would be gone.” finished Aaromir abruptly.

“Your right my lord,” began Adrastros, “our biggest concern right now is Ramigious. He is leading the Demarian forces in their center lines. So far, all attacks on that area have failed greatly. If we are to hit them in the critical area, I’d suggest attacking their center lines. The majority of their forces are located in that area.” added Adrastros.

Then Aaromir and the leaders gave the plan some thought

and worked it out. After reviewing the entire plan, Aaromir agreed to it. They then talked about what would happen if the Demarian center was to break.

"We would be able to cause a bulge in the Demarian lines and create a rift right in the center. Once that happens we would then send forces through the break and divide them to the east and west. This will allow us to outflank the Demarian lines and hit them from behind. Then we'll order our front lines to push forward and our units behind enemy lines to push inward.

With the enemy forces being hit from the front as well as from the back, their lines would break and retreat. Once that happens we'll carve a path straight to Demaria itself and drive deeper into the heart of the Demarian lands." concluded Aaromir. All the other leaders agreed without hesitation since this might as well turn the tide of the war and they couldn't even argue with the results that followed if the plan was a success. Also, since no one else had a better idea, the decision was pretty much unaminous.

"Very well then," agreed Aaromir, "I will send Aloysius out as soon as he returns."

"Excuses me lord Aaromir," objected Adrastros, "with all due respect, I am the only one who has fought Ramigious and seen first-hand the damage he and forces can inflict. I thought that I had put an end to that monster at the Olditron Canyons during our first encounter a decade ago. I lost a lot of good men that day and I plan to put a stop to his tyranny before he kills anymore of our brothers. That is why I am voluntarily and begging you to let me lead our forces against the Demarian center." begged Adrastros.

"Very well then, I'll let you lead our forces to attack the Demarian center," agreed Aaromir.

“Thank you my lord.” thanked Adrastros.

“Take as much men as you need and move out when you’re ready. Meeting adjourned.” ordered Aaromir.

After the meeting, Adrastros began to assemble an army. It took him three days to get it to the size he wanted, 900,000 Sinsorian swordsmen, pike men, and musketeers. He then set out with his army towards the great grassland of Phoenix. This was the largest army Adrastros had ever led in all his long 35 years of being leader. It was in Phoenix where this army would meet the largest Demarian force any of the men had ever fought throughout the five millennium war.

As the army entered the grasslands of Phoenix, they marched closely together. When the Sinsorians marched through half of the land, Adrastros held up his hand indicating them to stop. The men all looked ahead of them and saw the reason as to why they halted. In front of the Sinsorians was an army of 300,000 Demarians with Ramigious in front of them. The army was by far, the largest force any of them had ever seen before. They all knew, first hand, what a force of merely 10,000 demarians could do to an army of 100,000 Sinsorians. Pure carnage was the result as the Demarians had lost only 3,000 warriors while the Sinsorians lost 40,000 and were forced to retreat. Now the men were beginning to imagine the damage this army could inflict on them.

Some of the men took a step back and fell out of line. Adrastros noticed the men beginning to retreat and hollered at them to get back in line. The men got back into their original positions. Once the men were all in line, Adrastros nodded to musketeer who then fired a shot towards the Demarians. They waited a few seconds, and then suddenly a Demarian fell dead some 300 feet away. Then Ramigious and all the other Demarians looked at the dead Demarian then at the Sinsorians. They all pulled out their weapons and Ramigious pointed his sword at the Sinsorians, let out a scream, then they all charged right at them.

Adrastros saw the Demarians charging then yelled out "PIKE MEN!" The pike men then all appeared in front of him and lowered their pikes. Half kneeled while the rest stood with pikes extended. He then called out "SWORDSMEN!" and pulled out his blade. All the swordsmen did the same. The Demarians were now almost halfway across the grasslands when Adrastros called out, "MUSKETEERS!" and raised his sword. The musketeers raised their muskets and took aim at the charging Demarians.

"First line! FIRE!" cried Adrastros and aimed his sword at the Demarians. The first line of musketeers all fired and 3,000 demarians fell dead. "Second line!" and Adrastros lifted his left hand, "FIRE!" and flung his left hand down and another barrage of muskets fired into the Demarians and killed 3,000 more. Before the second line had fired, the 1st line of musketeers knelt down and began reloading. "Third line!" and the 2nd row of musketeers knelt down and began reloading. Adrastros had raised his sword again. "FIRE!" and a 3rd barrage of musket fire mowed down 3,000 Demarians.

By now the Demarians were halfway across the field. Adrastros then raised his sword and yelled" The rest of you," and all the musketeers raised their muskets and took aim. Then Adrastros screamed at the top of his lungs "FIRE!!" and thrust his sword in the air towards the Demarians. Every single musket went off simotanesly over the shoulders of all the Sinsorians and engulfed the army in smoke. Within the smoke Adrastros roused the men and yelled "FOR THE EMPEROR!!" and all the men let out a cheer and burst through the smoke, weapons drawn and charged at the Demarians. The Demarians had halted their charge since

10,000 of them had just fallen dead due to the last wave of musket fire.

Ramigious tried to fill the gaps in the line since the Sinsorian musketeers had killed so many Demarian warriors. He then saw the charging Sinsorians and ordered his army to charge. The Demarians took off full speed at the Sinsorians who were coming full speed at them. Within a few seconds, the two armies collided. The Sinsorian pike men ran full speed at the Demarians with their pikes extended. When the two armies collided, flesh was met by metal.

The pike men's long spears tore through the Demarian's chest and came through the other side. One pike men forced his spear into Demarian's chest, then jumped and forced him to the ground and impaling the spear into the ground. Another pike man managed to spear one Demarian. Then using the same spear, he ran until he tore through another Demarian then dropped the spear. Not all the pike men nailed a Demarian however. While a one pike man was charging, he tried to lunge his spear into a charging Demarian. The Demarian side stepped out of the way then grabbed the pike and pulled. The pull flung the pike man forward. The Demarian then elbowed him in the face, breaking his nose and forcing him to the ground.

The Demarian stood over the injured pike man and lifted his blade over his head. Just before he strikes, a spear is stabbed into his chest. The Demarian drops his sword and grabs the spear trying to pull it out. It was no use. Turns out a pike man had seen the Demarian elbow the other pike man and lift his sword over the injured pike man. So what this pike man did is run to his brother's aid. He stabbed his pike into the Demarian's chest and began running. His pike then impaled two more Demarians. When the third Demarian was impaled, he forced the pike further into the other two in front of him. The pike man then, using all his might, lifted the pike and forced it into the ground with all three Demarians through it, one on top of the other.

As the first pike man was getting up, a Demarian warrior came from behind him and stabbed his sword through his back and out his chest. The pike man placed his hands on the sword and gasped in pain. His pain was shortly lived. The Demarian then placed his massive hand over the pike man's face, and snapped his neck. After the Demarian withdrew his sword and let the lifeless body of the pike man fall to the ground, a swordsman came from behind and stabbed the Demarian in the back. The Demarian dropped to his knees in pain. Another swordsman came from in front of the demarian and shoved his sword into the Demarian's heart and the Demarian died and fell backwards. The musketeers were mowing down the demarians from a medley safe distance. One musketeer fired at a Demarian's head, killing him. Then another Demarian came from behind and, with his mace, struck the musketeer on the back of his head. The blow instantly incapacitated the musketeer and fell out cold on the floor. The Demarian then took two steps forward and smashed his mace on the musketeers head, hearing a crushing sound as his mace came in contact with the ground.

Ramigious was killing at will. He would side step a charging Sinsorians then slice him in the back. Then he would turn around and thrust his sword in the stomach of a musketeer, pull out his sword and slice a swordsman across the chest. A swordsman seen the carnage Ramigious was doing and ran right him. Ramigious had just sliced another swordsman when he saw the one charging at him. The swordsman slashed at Ramigious twice. Ramigious just stepped out of the way by moving to the right for the first slash and stepped to the left for the second slash. Then he grabbed the swordsman's head, forced him to bend to his side, and then kneed him in the ribs under his arm. The blow broke the Sinsorians's ribs and he let out a cry in pain.

Just then a swordsman and pike man who were nearby heard the scream and ran to their brother's aid. Once they saw Ramigious, they both charged at him. Ramigious saw them coming and prepared for a fight. He grabbed the pike man's pike and tugged it, forcing the pike man to fly forward. Then he stabbed the charging swordsman. He then pulled out his blade and grabbed the pike man by his shoulder and bent him back on to his knee. The pike man's upper back smashed on the impact of contacting Ramigious's knee. Ramigious then walked up to the swordsman who was still lying in pain grabbing his broken ribs. Ramigious lifted his sword and forced it into the swordsman's chest, ending his misery.

Adrastros was causing just as much harm as Ramigious. He would duck under a slash then lunge his sword into the Demarian's chest. He would then pull out his blade and block another slash. Then Adrastros would reverse the attack and slash the Demarian at his neck. Adrastros had just ducked another slash and sliced the Demarian who tried to slash him across his chest, when he saw Ramigious after the Demarian fell. Ramigious had just killed another swordsman, when their eyes met. For ten whole seconds they stared at one another motionless, while the fighting around them intensified.

Then Adrastros picked up his sword and charged at Ramigious screaming. Ramigious then charged at Adrastros and their swords clashed. They began striking at one another and during the entire time, Adrastros was thinking to himself:

"How could this be possible? I thought I killed him ten years ago. There must be some mistake. It must have been another Demarian. "Then Adrastros ducked under a slash and kneed Ramigious in the stomach and moved behind him and was about to stab him when he saw it. The opening in the back where his sword went through. He froze holding his weapon in stabbing position.

He then had a flashback and remembered that day. He specifically remembered himself stabbing Ramigious in the same spot he was looking at that same moment. As he was remembering all that went on he was interrupted in mid-thought with a punch from the back of Ramigious's fist to his face. When he came back to reality, Ramigious was fully turned around. He tried to slash Adrastros, but he stopped it in mid-air with his sword and forced it to the ground. Adrastros then withdrew his sword and stepped back in the nick of time, dodging an upward slash. Then he ducked under a sideways slash, feeling the air being compressed onto his face. Ramigious then swung his blade and Adrastros barley dodged it as he stepped backward. The sword cut a piece of Adrastros's hair that was flung in the air when Adrastros took his quick jump backward.

Adrastros saw the sword cut his hair as if in slow motion. He then tried to retaliate by swinging his sword at Ramigious. Ramigious blocked the sword swipe then moved his right hip to the left in time to dodge a stab by Adrastros. Ramigious then retaliated with a sword swipe of his own which was blocked by Adrastros. The two of them clashed swords for three minutes, each one blocking the others attack then trying to attack with their own strikes. Then the clashing finally stopped when Adrastros tried to slash Ramigious's head.

When Adrastros swung his blade, Ramigious blocked it with his blade. He then used all his might to force Adrastros's blade in a half-circle and pinned it down on the floor to his right. Ramigious then leaned back and smashed his left side into Adrastros. The blow knocked the air out of Adrastros and caused him to lose his grip on his sword and fall backwards. He landed hard and next to a dead Demarian. Ramigious then stood for a few seconds looking at Adrastros. He was lying helpless and defenseless on the ground. Ramigious knew that this was a golden opportunity and that he would not get another chance like this again. He began walking towards Adrastros, his sword in his left hand.

However, Ramigious's hesitation allowed Adrastros to catch his breath. He looked and saw Ramigious walking towards him. Out of the corner of his eye, he saw a Demarian blade. It was too late to reach for it however. Ramigious was now towering over him. Adrastros looked into the eyeholes of Ramigious's helmet and saw nothing more but utter blackness. Ramigious then grasped his blade handle with both hands and raised it above his head. Then he brought the blade down with all his might. While it was in mid-air, without hesitation, Adrastros reached over and grabbed the Demarian blade and turned back around and swung it, letting out a scream as he swung.

His main focus was to cut off Ramigious's arms. Instead, the blade missed both of Ramigious's arms and sliced him clear across the face from his lower left chin, diagonally across the face, to his upper right forehead, barley missing his eyes. When Adrastros sliced Ramigious's face, he lost control of his blade and instead of stabbing Adrastros in the chest, he went off course and sliced his right cheek with half a stab, cutting it open and turning Adrastros's face to the right. Ramigious was screaming in pain as blood dripped from his face. When Ramigious stabbed Adrastros, he too let out a scream in pain but only a little one. Adrastros, now aiming to capitalize on the situation, punched Ramigious in his bleeding face and forced him away from him.

Ramigious fell to the floor, still screaming in pain, and

placed his right hand on his face while gripping his weapon with his left. Adrastros quickly got up and grabbed his sword. Ramigious got up and tried to strike Adrastros (not knowing that he was already up). When Ramigious turned around, Adrastros stabbed him in his right hip. Ramigious then fell to the ground again as Adrastros pulled his blade out from his hip. Ramigious held his sword in his right hand and placed his left hand on his right hip as blood continued to spill from his face as well as his hip. Adrastros, looking to end it all right here, lifted his blade high above his head ready to strike a wounded, gasping, Ramigious on his back. Adrastros then brought his blade down with all his might.

Just as his blade was about to strike Ramigious, it stopped in mid-air, inches away from his back. A clash rang out. Adrastros looked to his right and saw a Demarian holding the blade that stopped his attack. Then a fist appeared in Adrastros's face out of nowhere. He backed up and placed his hand on his face. (Ramigious then began to crawl away while Adrastros was recovering from the punch). When Adrastros recovered from the punch, he looked forward and saw two Demarians with their weapons drawn.

Adrastros let out a small yell and charged at them. For a while they were able to block his attacks. Then Adrastros became frustrated and began screaming since he knew that the longer he fought them, the more time Ramigious has to recover, (little did he know that Ramigious had already crawled away to safety beyond the battle field). Adrastros then sliced one Demarian twice across his stomach. Then he ducked under a slash from the second one, moved behind him then stabbed him through the back and forced his sword through the front. Adrastros then let out a scream and turned around, and smashed his sword into the ground, believing that Ramigious was still there.

His blade cut through the air and smashed into the grass. Adrastros looked around for a limping Demarian. He only saw dead ones and his men pushing on. Infuriated that he had just missed his chance to kill Ramigious, Adrastros let out a scream in frustration and stabbed his sword in to ground. He continued to scream in anger as the battle waged on. Then after a few minutes, he picked up his sword and charged into the losing Demarians.

He killed hundreds of them in an effort to end his frustration. He was completely blood drunk. He let out a scream every time he swung his blade. The Demarians, now leaderless, tried to regroup and charge again. However, the Sinsorians musketeers were mowing down the regrouping Demarians. They left constant gaps in their lines. What's more is that the swordsmen and pike men kept on driving forward, killing more and more Demarians.

The Demarian lines broke and the Demarians scattered. This made them easy targets for the Sinsorians who pushed on and fought on until all the Demarians lie dead. Once the last Demarian fell, the Sinsorians all let out a huge cheer. Against their enemy's largest force, they have prevailed. Out of the 900,000 Sinsorians that charged into battle, 540,000 remained standing. Out of the 300,000 Demarians that charged into battle that day, only one remained standing. That one was Ramigious. He stood on the border of the Phoenix grasslands looking back from a hill, at the massacre sight. All of his warriors lie dead. He just put his head down and limped away into Demarian controlled land.

Out of all the cheering Sinsorians, Adrastros was the only one who was silent. Although he was glad and proud of his victory, he was still angry about not killing Ramigious. He then thought about what will happen now since the center lines of the Demarians had been broken. He then cracked a smile and looked northward to the border of the land. He then said cheerfully:

"You may have escaped me this time Ramigious, but soon you will have nowhere else to run to. We'll meet again someday soon, and when we do, I'll be ready and waiting."

CHAPTER 9

The Tide Turns

WITH THE VICTORY AT THE Phoenix grasslands, the Demarians were unable to support their front lines. Hundreds of thousands of Sinsorians and Trocarians poured through the gap in their lines. The Demarians front lines were engulfed and were completely wiped out. With the destruction of their front lines, everything went downhill fast for the Demarians. Since their front lines consisted of all their offensive units, the Demarians were now unable to push back or slow down the ever advancing Sinsorians. The deeper the Sinsorians pushed the lighter resistance they met. The

Demarians were now pulling back all available units to Demaria, where they would make their final stand.

With resistance weakening on all fronts, the Sinsorians fought harder. For they now knew very well that the war was finally coming to an end. Aaromir knew this as well and he planned to see it through. He used every bit of his power to make sure that the war did in fact come to an end. He did to the Demarians what they did to the Sinsorians. He began to split armies up and spread them out all around the land close to Demaria. Once Demaria was surrounded, he began to attack the Demarians from all sides. Surrounded and horribly outnumbered all the Demarians fell back to Demaria. The amount of Demarians in Demaria swelled from just a few thousand, to slightly over one million.

The Sinsorians continued to add pressure on the Demarians. They raided supply centers and occupied vital roads for troop transport. They even split the Demarians in the north from Demaria, cutting off all reinforcements and resources. Aaromir then sent an army of 50,000 to destroy the Demarians in the north believing that they are now weak enough to finish off, only one returned. He returned with some startling news.

"The Demarian numbers are still large my lord," claimed the survivor, "However they are not large enough to repel us forever. Another massive force should take care of them for good."

"No, they are no threat to us anymore," assured Aaromir, "they don't have the man power to launch an offensive, they can only defend. Although another force can get rid of them, I will not be sending one."

"Why not my lord?" asked the survivor.

"Because I will be needing everyman and Trocarian available to launch our final offensive to end this war." answered Aaromir gradually.

Aaromir's plan was simple, to hit the Demarians in Demaria from all sides with one huge attack. Aaromir himself was going to lead the men in their final battle for victory. The men were all extremly excited about it since it will be Aaromir's first time leaving the walls of Sinsoria in three millenniums. Aaromir's plan was to throw everything they had at the Demarians. He proclaimed, "None shall sit this one out. All shall partake in the largest battle in our empire's history. Though many shall fall, it will be a small price to pay for the reward we shall achieve, we have claimed…VICTORY!!!" These words of inspiration caused the men to let out a cheer every time they read or heard them.

The Demarians on the other hand were far from cheering. With the Sinsorians pushing in on all sides, their offensive ability had completely collapsed. Every army they sent out to slow down the Sinsorians never returned. Those that were able to stand and fight were defending Demaria. The armies placed at Demaria were willing to defend it until the last breath was exhaled from the last man standing.

Spehachor, on the other hand, did not plan to wait that long. He was on thin ice with the Demarians. They blamed him for all that has happened to them. (This was true since now he is banished from Sinsoria, forbidden to return on penalty of death). With each passing day, the Sinsorians moved closer and closer to Demaria. With every passing second, the hatred towards Spehachor grew larger and larger. The Demarians now viewed Spehachor as a liar and nothing more than dead weight. Day after day, the Demarians threatened Spehachor and day after day he thought harder about killing himself. Things were not getting better for him. Ramigious, now having healed and with new scars on his body, even threatened to snap Spehachor's neck if he didn't figure out a way to halt the Sinsorians advance.

Hoping to redeem himself and save his own life, Spehachor voluntarily decided to scout out a path through the mountains, behind the Sinsorians lines. Ramigious sent two Demarians with him, in case he tried to run away. They searched the mountains for three days and found nothing. Then on the fourth day, they stumbled upon a hidden cave. They followed it through hoping that it would lead behind Sinsorian lines. After eight hours of walking through the dark cave, they finally reached the end. Instead of having it open up behind Sinsorian lines, what it opened up to was far more valuable. This cave opened up directly under the throne room, in the heart of Sinsoria.

They may not break the Sinsorian lines, but they will be able to do what Spehachor said they were going to do, put an end to Aaromir's "rein". Spehachor and the Demarians ran back to Demaria and Ramigious. They told him about the cave and where it wound up. He immediately assembled an army of 500 of the greatest warriors in Demaria. Spehachor volunteered as well. They then set out and waited for the cover of darkness to deal the greatest blow to the Sinsorians ever since emperor Niastros's assassination, nearly eight thousand years ago.

CHAPTER 10

The Impalement of the Emperor

AFTER FOUR YEARS OF ADVANCING towards the heart of the Demarian war machine, the Sinsorians were now hours away. As they marched, they began to see the peeks of the mountains of Demaria. They continued to march onward. The Demarians began hearing the footsteps of the oncoming armies. Just when the Sinsorians were about to see the base of the mountains, they were ordered to stop. They stopped inches and seconds away from seeing the entire Demarian horde of one million warriors. The Sinsorians were confused about their sudden halt. When they asked Aaromir about why their advance had ground to a halt, he simply replied:

"All though we do outnumber our foes, they still have the strength to inflict massive deaths to our forces. So let us wait one more day to recover our strength and be well rested for our great battle. I also wish to spend one last night in Sinsoria before leading our forces, it might be my final night here, and it might not. The important thing is to be well rested and prepared for whatever happens tomorrow." Little did Aaromir know about what was going to happen tonight.

As the day dragged on, the Sinsorians along the front lines began preparing temporary camps for the night. They even set up guards and night watchers incase the Demarians tried anything funny. The Demarians held their ground the entire night. For they all knew about the small force moving into Sinsoria and if they held their ground, they hoped it would not arouse any suspicions. When darkness began to fall over the land, Ramigious and his small force of 500 Demarians began to move through the hidden cave. As the people of Sinsoria began to settle in for the night, Spehachor appeared in the exit of the cave.

After removing the boulder blocking the way, he poked his head out to look for any patrols. He seen one coming and immediately pulled it back in as the patrol passed by. One Demarian was about to strike at them when Spehachor stopped him and whispered "NO! You'll blow our cover." The patrol passed and Spehachor poked his head out and looked around, the coast was clear. He snuck out and backed up into the wall of a house. He again looked around, no more patrols passed by and the first one had just turned a corner and was headed in a different direction.

Then Spehachor motioned for the Demarians to come out of the cave. When they took their first step in Sinsoria, a sudden feeling came over them. They were instantly gripped by the need to pillage, destroy, crush, smash, and burn anything and everything they could get their hands on. The Demarians were able to shake off this feeling and move on. As soon as all of them were out of the cave, they headed towards the throne room.

When they reached the edge of a house that opened up into a wide street, Spehachor peeked his head over the corner. He saw the patrol that had passed walking away. Then something caught his eyes and made him hold his breath. He saw a Sinsorian swordsman coming in their direction. Spehachor immediately pulled his head back and drew his sword and pressed himself against the wall. The other Demarians did the same. As the swordsman approached and was about to turn the corner, Spehachor smacked his face with his sword handle and then grabbed him and threw his towards the Demarians. One covered the swordsman's mouth while the other stabbed him.

Spehachor again peered the corner and saw nothing but torches on their handles. Right when they were about to leave, Ramigious offered to stay behind and guard the entrance incase anymore patrols passed by. Spehachor agreed and warned him that he wouldn't be there when they kill Aaromir and continued to the throne room. Ramigious then dragged the dead swordsman into the cave and waited inside. Every now and again peering out on the lookout for more patrols.

Meanwhile, Spehachor and the other 500 Demarians had reached the entrance that led to the throne room. It was guarded by two guardsmen. These guardsmen were the elites of Sinsoria and were the best of the best when it came to fighting. They carried massive shields that protected them from thigh to neck. These shields were tipped at the top and curved into a wide body then reconnected at a tip in the bottom. Their spears were long poles that had a wide sword head for the spear head and had feathers sticking out where the stick met the sword. Their helmets had feathers made of metal at each side of the helmet and were almost full faced. There was a long metal line that ran down the center of the helmet and covered the nose and opened up all around the face. They wore a full set of body armor and a cape and followed the emperor everywhere he went unless he didn't require it.

These were the personal guard of the emperor and extremely hard to get passed in a frontal assault. Once Spehachor saw them, he knew they would not be easy to get passed. Thinking quickly, Spehachor decided to separate them and kill them sneakily. So he looked for something to use as a distraction. He found a water barrel a few feet from him. He used his sword to flip the barrel lid off which knocked over a metal container.

The guard noticed the container, just as Spehachor hoped; he looked at the other guard who nodded to him. Then he walked towards the barrel and turned the corner. Then there was the sound of a massive punch, a stab, and then the fall and sound of heavy metal hitting the floor. The second guard heard the fall and walked towards its source. When he turned the corner, there was a sudden bone snapping sound and the top torso of the guardsman fell in the wide street. He was then dragged out of sight and Spehachor's head popped from the corner.

Again, it was all clear and Spehachor motioned for the other Demarians to follow him. They then reached the stairway to the platform and ran up the stairs. When they reached the top, they saw more of the emperor's guard and a few Trocarians and Sinsorians. Realizing that there was going to be no sneaky way to get passed all of them, Spehachor decided to "turn himself in". When he walked towards the guards he yelled out:

“Hello boys! Was somebody looking for me?”

The guards yelled back:

“Freeze Spehachor!” and ran to confiscate his weapon. Right before they were going to take his sword away, Spehachor stabbed one of the guards and sliced a Sinsorians. Then he called out: “NOW!” and all the Demarians ran rushing towards the surprised guardsmen. They were completely baffled at seeing Demarians in Sinsoria.

“Demarians, here, HOW?!”

“Doesn’t matter just attack!”

The Demarians caught the guards by complete surprise and killed a few of them.

A group of 20 musketeers had heard the fighting from behind the throne room wall and ran up to investigate. When they saw the guards fighting the Demarians, they were baffled as well. They quickly shook the feeling off and began to fire. A swordsman tried to slice a Demarian near the edge of the platform. The Demarian grabbed the swordsman’s sword in mid-air with one hand, brought the Sinsorians forward and punched him in the stomach with the other hand. Then he kneed the swordsman in the face and threw him off the edge of the platform.

The swordsman plummeted 1,000 feet to his death. He was screaming the entire way and crashed into a food stand under the platform. A patrol was passing by when they heard the screams and the crash. They looked up to the platform and saw musket flashes and heard musket shots. They then immediately ran up to investigate and saw the fighting. They then charged into the Demarians to help their brothers.

As the fighting continued, Spehachor took 50 Demarians with him and ordered the rest to hold back the enemy. He and the 50 Demarians attacked the guards at the entrance of the throne room. As all this went on Aaromir was inside the throne room, clueless of what was going on outside. Then he heard: "STOP!" followed by the clashing of swords and tearing of flesh and the sound of his men dying. Aaromir was about to go outside to see what was going on when there was a sudden smash on the throne room door.

Aaromir then pulled back and heard another smash followed by a third smash. Aaromir pulled out his Sword of Kings expecting a fight. The smashing of the throne room doors continued until the doors broke off their hinges and Demarians came rushing through. One tried to slice Aaromir as he ran, but Aaromir ducked under the swipe and stabbed the Demarian in the back. Then he pulled out his sword and slashed another Demarian in the stomach.

He then brought back his sword and blocked a Demarian attack and forced their swords to the rock floor. Then Aaromir hit the Demarian with the back of his fist and slashed another Demarian in the stomach. One Demarian tried to stab Aaromir in his back. But Aaromir turned around, grabbed the Demarian's arm, and stabbed him in the side of the throat. Aaromir then withdrew his sword and turned around and sliced another Demarian and slashed another one. As Aaromir was killing off the Demarians, he was slowly moving forward.

Another Demarian tried to slice Aaromir, who ducked under the swipe and stabbed the demarian in the chest. Aaromir then withdrew his sword and ducked under a second swipe. Aaromir then took a step forward, rose, and threw his sword into a Demarian who had just entered the throne room. The sword landed in the neck of the Demarian and caused him to freeze and stand as straight as a tree. Aaromir then dodge rolled under a third swipe and stood up and grabbed his sword handle. He then swiped his sword to the right and cut it through the Demarian's throat and slashed three more Demarians across their chests with one swipe.

He then turned around and stabbed a Demarian, behind him, in the chest. A demarian from in front of Aaromir tried to slice his head, but Aaromir leaned back as the slash cut through the air and the Demarian slashed the Demarian, which Aaromir had just stabbed, in the throat. Aaromir withdrew his sword, grabbed the Demarian by his shoulder, and stabbed him in his waist. He then pulled out his blade, ducked under a fifth slash, side-stepped to the right, and leaped into the air almost 15 feet, and stabbed the Demarian in the throat. He then withdrew his sword, and while still in the air, stabbed another Demarian in the chest and forced it through him, which brought Aaromir crashing down on top of the sword handle. After a few more minutes of fighting, there were now only five Demarians left in the throne room.

The five Demarians gathered together and charged the emperor. Aaromir sliced one clear across his stomach and chest area once. Then he moved forward and sliced the second Demarian twice and moved forward again. Then Aaromir sliced the third Demarian three times and moved in again. When it came to the fourth Demarian, Aaromir ducked under a swipe then slashed the Demarian twice. The Demarian tried another slash and Aaromir ducked under it again and slashed him three more times. The Demarian, on his last bit of life, slashed again and again, Aaromir ducked under every slash. Then Aaromir began to slice in a continuous manner going faster and faster with every slice.

As Aaromir was slicing the fourth Demarian, Farah was approaching the throne room from behind. She was unaware of the fighting that was going on in and in front of the throne room. She was too busy practicing what she would say to the emperor to invite him to dinner. (No one had ever invited Aaromir to their house for a meal for as long as he has been emperor. It's not uncommon; the past four emperors have been invited to dinner by at least everyone once. It is only for Aaromir's time as emperor that he hasn't been invited since a lot has happened during his time on the throne. So Farah was going to be the first to invite Aaromir so this is a huge deal for her).

Meanwhile in the throne room, Aaromir's hand was now moving so fast, you couldn't even see his sword and arm anymore. All you could hear is the slicing of Aaromir's sword and the metal of the sword as it swiped through the air. Aaromir was moving his arm in a sideways 8 formation. Then just as quickly he had begun, Aaromir ended the swiping with a big slash and jumped forward. The Demarian remained where he stood, motionless. Then a drop of blood fell to the floor in front of the Demarian. Then two more fell next to the first drop and the Demarian collapsed forward. A pool of blood began to pour from his long dead body. In the end, Aaromir had sliced the demarian 300 times all over his body.

Now it was just Aaromir and the final Demarian. The Demarian attacked Aaromir with a slice, which he sidestepped out of the way from. Then the Demarian lifted his blade above his head and brought it down on Aaromir's head. Aaromir lifted his blade and blocked the attack in mid-air, half way from his head. Then Aaromir began to push his blade upward. The Demarian tried to push his blade down, but Aaromir was just as strong. They then found themselves in a test of strength.

Then a sword pierced Aaromir's back and he let out a scream in pain and lost his focus and grip on his sword. The Demarian quickly capitalized and pushed on his sword and forced the emperor to his knees. As soon as Farah heard the scream coming from the throne room, she quickly forgot what she was doing and immediately ran towards the throne room. When she made it to the front and saw the fighting, she let out a small gasp and placed her hands on her heart. Then she looked towards the throne room door and saw that it was burst open and the guards dead on the floor.

She ran towards the throne room and peeked inside. She saw Aaromir on his knees with a Demarian towering in front of him. She placed her hands on her mouth to hold back a scream. Then she ran back to get help. She saw a patrol walking and called out to them at the top of her lungs:

"GUARDS, GUARDS!!! It's the emperor he needs help!!!"

The guards looked towards the platform and saw and heard the musket fire and swords clashing. They immediately began raising the alarm and calling for everyone to come to the emperor's aid.

The alarm reached the Trocarians and Aloysius. They stepped out of the Solaris barracks and saw the muskets and fighting going on the platform. They then immediately ran to the emperor's aid. A massive line of Sinsorians and Trocarians ran passed Ramigious and the cave towards the throne room. As soon as they passed, Ramigious looked outside and saw the Sinsorians gathering in massive numbers and running up the stairs. He then knew that it was over and turned back, closed the cave exit, and headed towards Demaria. On the plate form, one pike man ran up and before he had a chance to attack, a Demarian ambushed him and threw him off the edge.

As the fighting intensified outside, things were not looking good for Aaromir. The stab had severely weakened him and the Demarian was pressing harder and harder. Then Aaromir gathered his strength and pushed back. He forced the

Demarian's sword to the side, leaving his entire chest wide open. Then Aaromir stabbed him in the heart with what strength he had left. When Aaromir pulled his sword out, he tried to get up. Just as he was about to get on his feet, a foot came out of nowhere and kicked the emperor in the face and forced him onto his back.

Then Spehachor stood towering above the wounded emperor. (Spehachor had snuck into the throne room and hid behind a pillar that held the ceiling of the throne room, and waited for the perfect time to strike. This was when Aaromir was in a test of strength battle with the Demarian).

"Look at every bodies favorite emperor now," mocked Spehachor, "you stupid pathetic waste!" and he kicked Aaromir in his ribs. Aaromir groaned in pain.

"I told you I'd make you pay!" and again kicked Aaromir, this time in the stomach. Aaromir again groaned in pain. He then saw his sword and began to crawl towards it. Spehachor seen him crawling towards the sword and went up to it and mocked: "Oh is this what you want?" and grabbed it by the handle.

Aaromir then forced himself up and stood on his knees in a daze. Spehachor then tried to stab Aaromir, but he blocked it and punched Spehachor. Spehachor then took a few steps back and wiped the blood from his mouth. He then looked at Aaromir, walked up to him, and punched him back. Aaromir fell to the floor and Spehachor proclaimed: "You don't know how long I've been waiting to do that!" then he threw Aaromir's sword aside.

Spehachor then saw a spear being held by one of the statues. He grinned manically and went up to it and began to pull it out of the statue's stone hands. As Spehachor pulled the spear, Aaromir gathered his strength and began to stand up.

When Spehachor had pulled the spear free, Aaromir was on his feet. Spehachor held the spear down and waited for Aaromir to look at him. When he did, Spehachor thrust the spear through Aaromir's heart. Aaromir let out a cry in pain and grabbed the spear, trying to pull it out. However, Aaromir was weakened from the stabs and blows he took and Spehachor still had strength to spare. He began to push the spear further into Aaromir's heart.

Aaromir then began to spin Spehachor, trying to throw him off the spear. Spehachor managed to fight through the spin and then began to push forward. He pointed Aaromir towards his throne and began to step forward as Aaromir stepped back. The closer they got to the throne, the harder Spehachor pushed on the spear. When they reached the throne, Spehachor used all his strength to push Aaromir onto the throne and drive the spear through him, into the stone of the throne. Aaromir was impaled to the throne of Sinsoria. His hands rested on the arm rests of the throne while his feet lay in front of it, as is he was just sitting on the throne like he does every day.

When Spehachor drove the spear through Aaromir, Aaromir let out a massive cry in pain. He was now impaled motionless to the throne. Spehachor went back for Aaromir's sword. As he approached Aaromir, he was unaware that the Demarians had now all been killed and the Sinsorians were heading to the throne room. Aaromir was helpless on the throne. When Spehachor reached him, he lifted his sword above his head and said: "Goodbye and good reddens." Aaromir closed his eyes as Spehachor drove the sword down.

Then a clash rang out. Spehachor stopped and looked on in disbelief. Aaromir then opened his eyes to find a halberd blocking Spehachor's strike. He followed the halberd to its source and found Aloysius standing next to him. Spehachor then looked at Aloysius, who with his other hand punched him in the face. The blow broke Spehachor's nose. Spehachor stepped back screaming in pain and gripping his nose. When he recovered, he lifted his sword above him and was about to strike when a hand grabbed his wrist.

Spehachor looked behind him to see a Trocarian grabbing his wrist causing him to drop Aaromir's sword. The Trocarian squeezed and broke Spehachor's wrist. Then Sinsorians came and grabbed Spehachor as well. They all then pulled out their swords and on the shadow on the wall, one can see them all stabbing Spehachor repeatedly. With Spehachor now dead, everyone now knew that he would not cause any more problems for the empire and bring no more harm to anyone else ever again. And the plague that had brought the empire to its knees, was now gone.

What Spehachor thought was Aaromir's heart was actually the area three inches above it. Spehachor had stabbed the vein that allowed for blood transfer to Aaromir's entire upper body. Luckily he missed the vein by a couple inches and has allowed for some blood transport. Although blood was being transferred to Aaromir's brain, it was only enough to keep it functioning. There was not enough blood to support the areas of the brain that allowed for motor function. Aaromir now has no control over his arms and legs. They are now forever, motionless on their position on the throne.

When the Trocarians and Sinsorians had finally killed Spehachor, they were heartbroken at what he did to their beloved emperor. Aloysius and the others tried to tend to the emperor. The first thing they tried to do was remove the spear. Since Aloysius was the leader of the Trocarians, he was the strongest of them. He tried to pull the spear out of the emperor. But the harder he pulled the more pain it brought to Aaromir. Upon hearing the emperor's cries of pain, Farah ran into the throne room and gasped at what she saw. To her, it looked as if Aloysius, her son, had stabbed the emperor.

When it was explained to her that Spehachor had done it, she began to shed tears. Although she was relieved over hearing that her son had saved Aaromir, she was crying over Aaromir. To see him in the helpless state that he was in made her feel torn up inside. The man that was supposed to be a symbol of strength, courage, and be a sparkling beacon of hope and leadership, was now nothing more than a body on an empty seat. As Aloysius tried to pry the spear from Aaromir, Aaromir was screaming in pain. The harder Aloysius pulled the greater pain he caused Aaromir, and the louder he screamed.

When Aloysius heard the emperor's screams, he began to cry as well. With each scream, Aloysius felt worse and worse about what he was doing. Even though he was trying to help, he was causing the emperor excruciating pain. That is something no one in Sinsoria can bare. To know that you are causing pain to someone who tried to prevent yours was unbearable to the people. Even if they were just trying to stop the emperor's pain.

After five agenizing minutes of trying to remove the spear, Aloysius gave up. Spehachor had jammed it in so well, it was impossible to pull it out. Aloysius blamed himself by saying that he was not strong enough. Aaromir tried to convince him that it wasn't his fault.

"It's not your fault," insisted Aaromir, "this spear was created to pierce the toughest armor. Only the one that created it would be able to remove it once it has pierced a surface. It is designed to stay within the surface it is thrust through until its creator, and only he, removes it. That is why the statue was holding it; the statue is the creator, well all that we have left to remember him." As the spear began to sink slowly back in, it brought the emperor mind numbing pain. It began to close off the oxygen and blood supply to the part in Aaromir's brain that allows him to speak. Luckily, Aloysius had pulled it out enough to ensure that Aaromir would be talk for a little while. Now as Aaromir talked, he began clenching between series of words, not all the time however.

"You mustn't "(clenches)"blame yourself" (clenches)" Aloysius," finished Aaromir abruptly. However Aloysius was in denial. He walked over to a table and flipped it over and then punched a pillar, sending multiple cracks through it, "Aaromir, if I had gotten here any sooner, you wouldn't be in the position you're in!" yelled Aloysius.

"Nevertheless if you had gotten here sooner than you might be the one on this throne instead of me!" Aaromir counter argued. Then he looked away and in a calm and relaxed tone, he looked back at Aloysius and said, "Aloysius, what's done is done, there is nothing you can do now later that will ever change it." Then in a more serious but relaxed tone he proclaimed, "As far as I'm concerned, we still have a war to finish."

Then Aloysius objected:

"My lord, we can't fight this war knowing that you're like this! What if something happens to you while we are all away? Who will help you?"

"You won't have to worry about me, I'm fine."

"But my lord you're not fine! Look at you!!" interrupted Farah.

"Listen!" yelled Aaromir, then he clenched again. Then again in a calm tone he said,

"It matters not if I am fine or not, all that matters now is ending this war. Since I am now unable to lead our forces, someone else will have to lead our forces and take my place on the battle field. Aloysius, it's going to have to be you."

"WHAT!" cried Aloysius, "ME I can't."

"Yes, you can, I believe in you."

"No Aaromir you don't understand, I…I can't lead an army that size."

"Yes you can, you led the Trocarians, why should this be any different?"

"My lord that's a whole different topic. I only led single armies of Trocarians, usually a maximum number of 50,000."

"So what's the difference now?"

"The difference is that this time, I will be leading multiple armies of Trocarians and armies of Sinsorians that I have never led before. Not to mention that the number this time is not 50,000, but 5.5 million soldiers of Trocarians and Sinsorians alike. I can't do it!"

"Aloysius, if I didn't think you could lead this army, and then I would have never let you lead the Trocarians. I specifically chose you since I saw the potential of a great leader. Every leader has his moment where his skills and abilities to lead will be tested. This is your moment. Prove to me that I made the right decision in appointing you leadership. Now is the time to show your strength. Now is the time to prove to me and everyone else that it was not a mistake appointing you leadership. Will you rise to greatness or fall into darkness?"

Aloysius then stopped and thought about what Aaromir said. He reviewed the words in his mind as they spun wildly around. He then turned and faced his mother. She was looking at Aaromir and agreed with his point. She then looked at her son and nodded with a tear. He then nodded back and turned to face Aaromir.

"I'll do it," he proclaimed.

"Excellent," agreed Aaromir, "you will have until dawn to ready the men. Good luck."

Then all throughout the night Aloysius went around Sinsoria spreading the word on what had happened to the emperor.

At first, the men were in disbelief. Some went to see for themselves, and when they did, their hearts sank. Their first thought was:

"How can we go on without the emperor leading us every step of the way?" Their first feeling was anger. Like Aloysius, they blamed themselves for not being there when the emperor needed them. Aloysius explained to them that the Demarians were to blame for all that has happened. He tried to rouse the men so that they would fight by his side. However, the men were hit hard by the news and it needed time to sink in. After hours of trying to gather the men, Aloysius began to give up. He began to think that the men would be too preoccupied doubting themselves than fighting to end the war. Just as the sun began to peek over the horizon, Aloysius gave up on the men.

Right when Aloysius was getting ready to tell Aaromir that he won't be able to lead the forces, he was stopped by Adrastros.

"Aloysius! Where do you think you're going?" questioned Adrastros, "We have a war to win."

"It's no use Adrastros. The men cannot fight. Thcy are too busy blaming themselves for the actions of the enemy."

"I wouldn't tell the men that."

"Why not?"

"Because they don't look preoccupied to me."

Just then, Sinsorians and Trocarians appeared all around Aloysius and Adrastros. They all had their weapons and armor ready and they looked ready for a fight. Aloysius looked around and admired the men and Adrastros most of all, who had convinced the men to fight. Then Kenneth of the royal and town guards proclaimed:

"If the enemy wants to try to assassinate our emperor on our land, and slays our brothers on our land, then that makes it personal!" The Sinsorians and Trocarians then all let out a cheer. Adrastros then called out:

"UP MEN!!!! TO DEMARIA!!!!"

The men let out another cheer and began marching.

As the sun rose higher above the horizon, dawn finally came. When the sun shine hit the Sinsoria, the gates opened and Aloysius marched through them. Behind him was Adrastros and the other leaders. And behind them, were all the Sinsorians and Trocarians of Sinsoria. All 5.5 million of them.

As they marched towards Demaria, they were joined by other armies of Trocarians and Sinsorians. This was the first time the Sinsorians and Trocarians had ever marched together under a single leadership. Although they do end up in the same battle most of the time, they never enter it together. After three hours of steady marching, the army had finally reached Demaria and joined the front lines and armies waiting there. By this time, the army had swelled in size and number. With every step taken, the ground shook and the sound of marching echoed throughout the land.

Meanwhile at Demaria, the Demarians were preparing for their final stand. They had poured as many warriors as can be stuffed into Demaria. A force of nearly 600,000 soldiers. However, with the news of the failed attempt to kill the emperor, the Demarian hopes of turning the tide of the war were dashed and gone. Now they can only defend their home, against an ever approaching army, for as long as they could hold out. The Demarians had managed to do some recruiting and managed to create 500,000 additional raw recruits. The force defending the entrance of Demaria was now 1.5 million soldiers. Each of them ready to defend it until the end.

It was all quiet at the entrance of Demaria. The Demarians were enjoying one last nap before the battle that will decide their fate would take place. All the Demarians slept peacefully as the hours passed. Then there was a sudden shake, then another. It was faint, but it grew fiercer with every passing second. When the vibration began to move pebbles and small rocks around, the Demarians began to wake up. Then they heard the sound. Although it was distant, they could clearly make out what it was. They all stood up and drew their weapons. They then began to group together to secure their flanks. Ramigious then took the lead at the front of the army.

The sound and shaking grew louder and fiercer as time slowly passed. The sound then echoed throughout the walls of Demaria. The Demarians then began to look around in all directions. The sound was coming from all around them. Ramigious held his glare and head facing forward. Then a thin line of sunlight appeared across the horizon behind the hill in front of the Demarians. The Demarians then all began to face forward. They lifted their weapons and gripped them tightly with both hands. With every passing second, the sunlight grew brighter and brighter as the sun rose higher in the sky.

The sound grew louder and louder as its source grew closer and closer. Then it suddenly stopped just as quickly as it came. That's when they all knew…their enemy has finally arrived. After five minutes of waiting, a figure began to appear on top of the hill. As the figure walked further up the hill, the Demarians could see that the figure was a man. The further the man walked up the hill, the brighter the sun grew behind him and the clearer his image became. When the man stopped at the top of the hill, the sun was shining in the Demarian's eyes. Through the sunshine, they saw Aloysius standing on top of the hill.

Then Ramigious let out a scream and as soon as he did that, all the other Demarians began to scream as well. They pounded their fists on their breast plates and raised their weapons in the air. They were trying to show their enemy that they were not afraid and were ready for a fight. Just then, Adrastros and the other leaders showed up behind Aloysius. The Demarians continued their screaming and pounding. Then the Sinsorians and Trocarians showed up behind their leaders, cheering as they appeared on top of the hill.

As more and more Sinsorians and Trocarians appeared on top of the hill, they began to spread out in a long line. When the Demarians, saw the increasing number of enemies, they began to quiet down and stare in disbelief. When all the Sinsorians and Trocarians had appeared, their numbers were an astonishing 6.5 million. The Demarians were now literally outnumbered 5:1. Just as the Demarians were in disbelief of the Sinsorians and Trocarian numbers, the Sinsorian and Trocarians were just as shocked at the Demarian numbers.

As the two forces stared down one another, Adrastros said, more to himself than anyone else, "So many." The other leaders nodded in agreement. Just then the Sinsorians and Trocarians began to fall out of line. None of them had ever fought an army this large before for as long as the war dragged on. Even though Adrastros had led an army of 900,000 to fight an army of 300,000 Demarians which was the largest force a single army had ever fought. There had only been a few occasions in the war where multiple armies had ever faced off, however, the Demarian numbers hardly topped 250,000.

When the leaders saw the men falling out of line, they began yelling and ordering them to get back in line, all of them except Aloysius. He held his ground staring at the Demarians. Who he was staring at was Ramigious. He easily singled him out due to the massive scar across his helmet, from the bottom of his left chin, to the top right side of his forehead. Ramigious stared back at him, as if each tried to read the others mind. After 30 seconds of staring at one another, Ramigious turned around to deal with his forces.

Aloysius then continued to stare and thought to himself:

"What am I doing here?"

When he turned around to look at his forces, he got his answer. He looked upon the men's faces, and what once had been anxiety, was now fear. As the men continued to fall out of line and the leaders trying to keep them in line, Aloysius had finally realized what he had to do.

"TROCARIANS!!! SINSORIANS!!!!!" screamed Aloysius. Everyone stopped what they were doing and looked at him.

"My brothers! Stand your ground and hear what I have to say," he ordered," Our enemy stands before us, cowering in front of us. But here I see you cowering in front of them. Tell me, what good does it do to cower in front of fear? As I look upon your faces, I see something that I have not seen in over two decades, FEAR!" As Aloysius talked, he used hand motions and looked at the men.

“I see in your eyes the same fear that would take the heart of me! The enemy believed that by impaling our emperor, they would crush our spirit and will to fight. But look who stands before them today!” Aloysius raised his halberd and all the Sinsorians, and only the Sinsorians, let out a massive cheer and got back in line.

“There our enemy stands,” (Aloysius points at the Demarians), “the sheer nightmare that they are. The nightmare that has brought pain, suffering, and death to our people. I shall fight it! WHO shall fight with ME!!?” (Then Aloysius raised his halberd and began running to the side screaming), “WHO SHALL FIGHT WITH ME!!!” This time all the Trocarians, and only the Trocarians, let out a massive cheer and got back in line. Aloysius's main goal was to rouse both the Trocarians and the Sinsorians at once.

Then Adrastros proclaimed:

“I am with you until the end my brother!” and drew his sword. The other leaders pulled out their swords as well.

“Come my brothers!” called Aloysius, “Let us end this war and nightmare today! For the empire! For the emperor! For Sinsoria! And for AAROMIR!!!”

Then all the Trocarians and all the Sinsorians, together, let out a cheer that shook the ground and charged full speed at the Demarians.

When Ramigious saw the Sinsorians and Trocarians charging, he lifted up his sword and let out a scream and pointed his sword at the charging men. The Demarians let out a scream as well and charged. Now both armies were charging at one another with no intentions of turning back. As the armies grew closer to one another, the anger and hatred of 5,000 years of war could be felt as the fate of an entire race hung in the balance. The men all screamed as they charged. When the armies were about 100 feet from one another, it suddenly grew silent. No noise was heard even as the armies charged. Although the men's mouths were open, no sound was coming out. It was all dead silent.

Within a matter of seconds the silence was broken by the massive of the armies colliding. The sound was so massive that it echoed throughout all of Demaria. Men flipped, Demarians flew, and shields were smashed upon impact. One Trocarian smashed his shield into a Demarian and used it to flip him. Then with sword in hand, he slashed one Demarian, then brought it back and cut one across the throat. He then blocked and attack and slashed the Demarian, who tried to attack him in the stomach.

Then, using his shield, he deflected an attack and punched the Demarian in the face, smashing his helmet. He then used his elbow to smash the helmet of the Demarian behind him. The Trocarian then stabbed another Demarian, and with one arm, lifted him into the air, with the sword still inside of him, and brought the Demarian over his head and stabbed the sword into the ground behind him. The Trocarian then turned around and bashed a Demarian with his shield. He then bashed another Demarian with his shield and blocked an attack from a different Demarian, then using both hands to snap the Demarians neck sideways. He then used his battered shield to smash one last Demarian, before letting it slide off his arm on impact. Weaponless now, the Trocarian continued to fight.

Using only his hands he punched one Demarian with his right hand, and another one with his left. With both punches, he bashed in their helmets. One Demarian tried to smash the Trocarian's helmet with his sword handle. But the Trocarian blocked the Demarian's arms and forced them behind the Demarians head. Then he used his foot to trip the Demarian and then deliver the finishing punch that smashed the Demarian's helmet. Another Demarian tried to stab the Trocarian, but he stepped out of the way, stole his sword, and used it to slit the Demarian's throat.

He then turned around and stabbed another Demarian, slashed a second one, sliced a third one, and finally stabbed the blade into the side of the neck of a fourth and final Demarian. Then three Demarians came and stabbed their weapons into the Trocarian's stomach, while a fourth one came and sliced the Trocarian's in the throat, putting an end to the Trocarian's killing spree. In the end, the Trocarian had an astonishing, 18 kills, which was more than what any other Trocarian and Sinsorian can dream of getting. As the fighting continued and began to intensify, the knights led by Borachius, charged into the Demarian flanks. 300,000 on the right flank and 300,000 on the left flank. With the Demarians being attacked on all fronts and had nowhere to else to go, they stuck to their promise. They continued fighting until the last man standing.

Even though the Demarians were immensely outnumbered, they knew that if they retreated, all of Demaria will fall. So they held their ground and continued to fight. After three hours of fighting, the men began to gain the upper hand in the battle. To add more pressure on the losing Demarians, the musketeers moved from the rear of the army to the open flanks and began firing at the rear of the Demarian force and at any Demarian who found himself without anybody to fight. This tactic was ordered by Adrastros and it began to increase the amount of Demarian deaths. It also cut off any reinforcements from Demaria. It also allowed the Sinsorians to encircle the losing army.

Meanwhile at the heart of the action, Aloysius was hacking away at the Demarians. He had just hacked a Demarian in his head, hearing his skull crack, and forced him to the ground. When the Demarian fell, Ramigious came into view. Aloysius saw him, slaughtering his men. Ramigious slashed one Sinsorian swordsman, then sliced a Trocarian, and stabbed a Sinsorian pike man. Upon seeing this, Adrastros lifted his halberd and ran screaming towards Ramigious. Ramigious had just finished killing a musketeer when he heard Aloysius's screams. He turned and ducked just in time to miss a swing of the halberd. However, when Aloysius swung his halberd, he managed to hack a Demarian who was behind Ramigious.

Aloysius then swung his halberd back as Ramigious rose. Ramigious moved his head back, barely missing the swing. He then took another step back, dodging a third swing. He then swung his sword at Aloysius, who then blocked it with his halberd handle. Then Adrastros saw Aloysius fighting Ramigious and rushed to his aid. Aloysius then pushed Ramigious away and tried to hack his head. Ramigious then side stepped out of the way missing the smash. Then Aloysius smacked Ramigious with the back of his fist, causing him to turn around in a daze.

Ramigious quickly came to and was able to block an attack by Adrastros. Then Ramigious took a few steps back and examined his foes. Then Aloysius and Adrastros attacked Ramigious together. They used each other to defend one another and attacked together. Aloysius would swing; Ramigious would block the swing then attack. Aloysius would duck under the swing and Adrastros would block it then use Aloysius as a surface, climb onto his back and leap into the air and attack Ramigious. Ramigious would then block the attack and step back. These types of tactics were used against Ramigious for a few minutes.

Then Ramigious realized that he could not fight both of them at once. So when Adrastros attacked, Ramigious blocked the attack and grabbed Adrastros's sword. Then he kneed Adrastros in the stomach, knocking the wind out of him, and head butted him in the head, knocking him out cold. Then he threw Adrastros's unconscious body aside and faced Aloysius. Then Ramigious attacked Aloysius. Aloysius blocked the swing with his halberd, and punched Ramigious. Ramigious then retaliated with a punch of his own, then a back fist.

Then he grabbed Aloysius and kneed him in the gut. He then lifted his face and punched him in the nose, breaking it and also managed to punch Aloysius in the mouth, causing him to bleed. The blow to the face dazed Aloysius and caused him to step back. He put his hand to his face and brought it back to see his own blood. Angered at the sight of his own blood Aloysius ran at Ramigious and tried to attack him. Ramigious managed to grab the halberd handle and forced Aloysius towards him. Then he kneed Aloysius again and with his sword handle, smashed Aloysius in the back and forced him to the ground.

Then Ramigious grabbed Aloysius and threw him aside. Aloysius landed hard on the floor and turned on his stomach. Ramigious then saw a golden opportunity. With his sword in the hand he began to walk towards Aloysius. Aloysius managed to get up on his hands and knees. He heard Ramigious coming and grabbed his halberd and gripped it tightly. Ramigious then stopped behind Aloysius and grabbed his sword handle in both hands and began to raise his blade into the air. By this time, Adrastros was beginning to regain consciousness.

As Ramigious held his sword in the air, Aloysius was waiting for the right time. Then the time came. When Ramigious brought his sword down, Aloysius lifted his halberd, screamed a little and turned around. His halberd smashed into Ramigious's stomach, causing his stab to go off course and slice Aloysius across his back. Aloysius let out a swift cry in pain then withdrew his halberd. Ramigious fell to his knees as Aloysius rose and stood beside him.

Ramigious placed his hands on his stomach then took it off and looked at his own blood. Aloysius lifted his halberd high into the air, let out a scream and brought it into the front of Ramigious's neck. The halberd then sliced through the air, blood stained. Then Adrastros had finally become conscious and grabbed his weapon. He then stood and turned around, ready to fight. Right when he turned around, Ramigious's head bounced towards him and stopped with his eyes staring at Adrastros. Adrastros looked at the head, and then looked at the headless body of Ramigious fall forward. He then saw Aloysius breathing heavily and with a bloody nose and mouth. He then nodded towards him and he nodded back.

By this time, the Demarian force was completely surrounded on all sides and dying out quickly. Now leaderless, the Demarians fought on blindly. It was now everyman for himself. Upon seeing Aloysius and Adrastros work together to kill an enemy, the Sinsorians and Trocarians began to work together as well. One Demarian knocked a Sinsorians down and was about to stab him when a Trocarian came from the side and bashed his shield into him. Another Trocarian was killing a Demarian when one came from behind him. He was about to slice the Trocarian in the back when a pike man threw his spear into the Demarian. After three more hours of fighting, the Demarian force of 1.5 million warriors was no more. Then the Sinsorians musketeers began unleashing massive barrages of musket fire into the gateway of Demaria, killing thousands and creating a path for the rest for the men.

When the musketeers had killed 300,000 Demarians, the rest of the Trocarians and Sinsorians ran through the gateway and stormed the land. Within a matter of hours, all the

Demarians were slaughtered and after five millenniums of war, Demaria had finally fallen. With the fall of Demaria, the Sinsorians and Trocarians all let out a massive cheer. They now claim victory over their fallen foes, but at a price. Out of the 6.5 million warriors that charged into battle that day, 4 million remained standing to celebrate the end of the war,

For there, on that historic day, under emperor Aaromir's leadership, the Sinsorians and Trocarians claimed victory and declared an end to the war. When the news reached Sinsoria, all the towns people let out a massive cheer and began to cry. Only this time, the tears they were crying were not tears of sorrow or misery, but tears that no one had seen in a long time. These were tears of joy. All the Sinsorians, Trocarians, and towns' people welcomed the new era of peace they had long fought and died for. However, their only regret is that they cannot celebrate it with the man responsible for bringing it to them, emperor Aaromir.

With the emperor impaled to the throne of Sinsoria, he was unable to enjoy the peace that has finally come. Throughout the long history of the war, billions were lost. Among those billions were the four emperors who led the people through it all. However, with Aaromir impaled to the throne only one thought runs through the minds of the people now. And that is: if they are going to have to enjoy this peace with or without him.

The Ambush

WITH THE WAR FINALLY OVER, all the men in Sinsoria did what they never did before during the war or even the five year waiting period, and that is, they hung up their armor, put away their weapons, and spent the rest of their lives with their families. Although Demaria has fallen into Sinsorians hands, and all the Demarians in the mainland had been killed, the Demarians in the northern volcanic lands (the Black Lands) still posed a threat. However, their numbers are too small to mass an attack on Sinsoria itself, let alone a base or supply center. To make sure that they don't pose a threat to the empire or its people, Aaromir doubled the size of the units protecting the military bases and supply centers near the volcanic lands. These forces met with massive offenses and stiff heavy resistance for seven months.

After the seven months had passed, the Sinsorians held their ground and trapped the remainder of the Demarians in the northern lands. Even though the main and back up armies had put away their weapons and were enjoying a life of peace and solitude, there were resistance groups all throughout the empire. Now these resistance groups are lead by Adrastros. They are made up of single men, disowned members of families, men whose wives had left them, men who lost their wives, fresh recruits, or very great war mongers. These men were all loyal to the emperor. Their resistance is towards the peace they have achieved. They will not be fully satisfied with it until all Demarians are dead and swept right off the face of the planet.

The resistance groups simply refer to themselves as "The Resistance". Aaromir has allowed them to use any resource they wish to finish off the Demarians. Their numbers are not very large. Probably about 20 to 25 thousand men max. Not even a quarter of a fraction of the Sinsorian main force. The resistance attacks the Demarians in small groups of up to 25 to 30 men per group. They don't send all their force at once since the Demarians had been spread all about the land. Making it ripe for ambushes in nearly all directions.

The resistance has only one rule: fight until the last man standing. With this rule in mind, the resistance sends out its small attack forces, most of which never return. This is okay since with every man that dies, a Demarian dies as well. With every Demarian killed, their chances of survival grow dimmer and dimmer. Now Adrastros leads his party into the lands, completely clueless of what shall become of him and his men.

As the party moved further into the northern lands, they began to see remnants of old skirmishes. Heaps of bodies piled onto one another, both Sinsorians and Demarians alike.

The men kept on moving forward, now with revenge on their minds. As they walked, a light fog began to creep in. The deeper in the men moved, the denser and thicker the fog became.

Fearing that they might lose one another in the thickening fog, the men all huddled together. Adrastros kept his pace ahead of the group. He was only about five footsteps ahead of the men, and they could hardly see him. They kept their steady pace until the fog seemed to lighten up as they approached an empty arena. The arena was riddled with the remains of dead soldiers from battles and skirmishes long passed.

"Where are they?" asked Kenneth, one of the royal and town guards, "We should have met them by now."

"Calm yourself Kenneth, they're here," assured Adrastros. After five more minutes of marching, the fog had lifted enough so that the men could now see each other clearly. Then the men reached the center of the arena when Adrastros held up his hand, indicating to the men to stop.

Even though the fog had lifted a little, the area around the small group was covered by a thick fog. Adrastros had thought that he had heard something and began to look around. When he was almost done with his search, something out of the corner of his eye caught his attention. When he looked, he saw him. A lone Demarian standing 20 feet away from him. Adrastros placed his hand on his sword handle and was about to pull out his sword when another Demarian came out of the fog and stood next to the first one, then another, and another, and another.

Demarians came out of the fog in all directions and soon enough, the men found themselves completely surrounded and outnumbered on all sides. The men drew their weapons and moved closer together in battle stances. The musketeers took aim and waited for the order. Then Adrastros called out:

"MEN OF SINSORIA", and pulled out his blade and raised it into the air," FOR THE EMPEROR!" Then Adrastros ran at the Demarians, his men followed and screamed as they ran.

One Demarian lifted his blade to his side ready for an attack. Adrastros then sliced the Demarian in the stomach and the men collided. The Demarians began slicing and hacking away at the Sinsorians. One musketeer fired at the head of one Demarian, killing him. Then another came from the side and smacked the musket out of the musketeers hands and elbowed him in the face, knocking him to the floor and then stabbed him to finish him off. One swordsman managed to duck under a mace swing from a Demarian. The Demarian then quickly turned around and smashed the swordsman's legs. The smash to the legs tossed the swordsman into the air, and then while in mid-air, the Demarian smashed his mace on the swordsman's head, hearing the skull cracking when the mace came in contact with the ground.

A second musketeer fired at another Demarian, when one came from behind, placed his hand on the musketeer's shoulder, then stabbed his sword though his back and forced it through the musketeer's chest, blood stained. The musketeer was gagging and gasping in pain as he placed his hands near the sword. Then the Demarian withdrew his blade and threw the musketeer aside and went after the next one. Meanwhile, while his men were dying, Adrastros was killing at will. He would duck under a sword swing, grab the Demarian's arm, and then stab him in the waist.

He would then pull out his blade and block the attack of a second Demarian, and slice him across his chest. His killing spree would end when he attacks a third Demarian. Adrastros would duck under the Demarian's swipe and attack his legs. He would use all of his might to launch the Demarian into the air then, while he is still in the air, Adrastros stabbed his sword into the Demarian's chest and forced him in the ground. When Adrastros pulled his sword out and rose, he saw his men losing badly. When he tried to rouse them, a Demarian came from behind and hit him on the back of the head.

The blow dazed Adrastros and caused him to fall. When Adrastros fell, he let go of his sword. When Adrastros recovered, he tried to grab his sword and continue fighting. When he grabbed the handle, a Demarian placed his foot on Adrastros's sword, preventing him from lifting it. Adrastros looked at the Demarian, who then punched him in the face. The punch knocked Adrastros back and caused him to release his grip on the sword handle.

Just then, Kenneth tried to rise to save his leader, a Demarian shoved his sword into Kenneth's back and forced him to the ground. When Adrastros looked in front of him he saw two things. The first was the blood stained tip of the blade that had stabbed Kenneth. And the second thing was a Demarian making his way towards him, with his sword drawn. Adrastros tried to get up, but a Demarian came and held him down with his foot. The Demarian then stopped in front of Adrastros and raised his blade.

When the Demarian was about to strike, Adrastros saw his entire life flashing before his eyes then a musket shot rang out. A split second later, nearly half of the Demarian's face blew off. He wobbled then fell backward. As he fell, 20 Sinsorians charged at the Demarians and began to kill them off. The charging Sinsorians had just fought off a Demarian ambush nearby when they heard the fighting going on where Adrastros was located. They came running just in time to save Adrastros.

The Demarian who was holding Adrastros down took his foot off to go fight the oncoming Sinsorians. Adrastros then leapt for his weapon while the Demarians were occupied and he escaped. When he got to a nearby cliff, he stopped and looked back. He saw the Sinsorians being slaughtered by the Demarians. He was glad to be alive, but he was also devastated for his lost men. Then he thought to himself and cracked a smile.

"So long as there is still a Demarian who draws breath here, I shall continue to return." He proclaimed allowed to himself. Then he turned and headed for Sinsoria.

CPSIA information can be obtained at www.ICGtesting.com
Printed in the USA
LVOW132021101212

311011LV00001B/19/P

9 781457 510434